nificent book and I hope to see these characters again in the future."

—Victoria *Cocktails and Books*, 5 Stars

"I really enjoyed this book and the characters! Sexy story with a great message, would definitely recommend!"

—Casey *Ramblings From This Chick* 4 Stars

Other Titles by Anne Lange

THE VAULT SERIES
FRIENDS WITH BENEFITS
HERS TO OWN
WICKED INDULGENCE
WHO'S THE BOSS?

A NEW LEAGUE SERIES
SLIDING INTO HOME
THE FINAL QUARTER

FAMILY TIES
HER CHOICE

ANTHOLOGIES
THE PERFECT MOMENT
(*A SHORT STORY IN THE VAULT SERIES*)
(*PART OF THE VALENTINES HEAT IV ANTHOLOGY*)

PRAISE FOR ANNE LANGE

FOR *FRIENDS WITH BENEFITS*

"What a nice ménage romance! All three main characters were lovable. I definitely recommend it."

—*Mary's Ménage Whispers*

"The best part about this book? It also has a real story going on in between the sex scenes. Friends with Benefits is emotional, heartwarming, anger evoking, thought provoking, passionate and sigh worthy."

—Robin, *Book Reads and Reviews*

"Ms. Lange's writing is fluid, solid, and incredibly hot. I was fanning myself the entire time I read this...her word choice and narrative had me fully in the moment. There is real depth in the love that builds between Tyler, Angela, and Connor."

—Author Erin Moore

"This story has everything you'd want from a sexy ménage. Smoking hot chemistry, panty melting sex and down-home relatable characters."

—Author Renea Mason

FOR *WORTH THE RISK*

"Worth the Risk is my first book by Anne Lange and I loved it. ...[I]t piled on the personality and hot scenes. I never felt like anything was being rushed along because of the length of the book. If you are looking for a sweet, fun, hot read to pass a few hours this is the one for you."

—Tina *Coffee and Books* 4.5 Stars

"A smoothly-written and well-executed erotic romance novel, Worth the Risk immediately captures the reader's attention and emotions and maintains that grasp throughout until the ending, leaving the reader to relax in satisfaction with a 'well done!' to the characters and the author."
—*Mallory Heart Reviews* 5 Stars

"As Molly and Tanner reunite through numerous steamy sexual encounters (and there are A LOT of encounters) we get brief glimpses of a fun and supportive group of friends and I was intrigued by all of them. It was easy to immerse myself in this story as each member of the group was easy to relate to. Ms. Lange has created a wonderful hero and sets us on an emotional roller coaster ride that ends in an immensely satisfying conclusion. So take a risk and read Worth the Risk."
—*J.Faltys' Words of Wisdom....from The Scarf Princess*

FOR *HERS TO OWN*
"I really enjoyed reading this book, it was fun and had some thrill. It's not your typical romance story which is why I think it works. It not only deals with BDSM but body image and what you can do to get over a bad body image and tell yourself not only are you beautiful but believe it as well. I recommend this book with immense pleasure."
—Wild Rayne *Night Owl Reviews Top Pick* 4.5 Stars

"I found this book well written with a fascinating plot. The main characters and the secondary characters were interesting. This book does a great job of keeping the reader on the edge of your seat as each twist and turn unravel. I had a hard time putting this book down. Overall, this was a very mag-

Her Choice

FAMILY TIES, BOOK 1

ANNE LANGE

hotRom publishing
OTTAWA, ONTARIO

Her Choice
Family Ties, Book 1
Copyright © 2016 by Anne Lange. All rights reserved.

Her Choice is a work of fiction. All names, characters, businesses, places, events and incidents are either the product of the author's imagination or used in a fictitious manner and are not to be construed as real in any way. Any resemblance to persons, living or dead, actual events, locales, or organizations is entirely coincidental. All trademarked marked items are assumed to be the property of their respective owners and are used only for reference.

Published By hotRom publishing
105 Porcupine Trail, Ottawa Ontario, Canada, K0A1T0
ISBN: 978-0-9939695-3-9

Editing by Red Pen Coach
http://www.theredpencoach.com/
Cover Photo by Jenn LeBlanc / Illustrated Romance
https://illustratedromance.com/stock-images/
Cover Design by EDH Graphics
http://edhgraphics.blogspot.ca/
Book Layout and Design by Ryan Fitzgerald
http://ryanjamesfitzgerald.ca

Due to the dynamic nature of the Internet, website links contained within this book may be outdated and/or no longer valid.

Revision: June 2016

Dedication

Thanks to my brand new beta reading crew, Julie, Haidee and Sharon.

This one is for you.

You're the first readers to see this brand new story, and the first to tell me I did good when I was nervous about taking this slightly different step.

It's got a lot less sex than usual!

Thank you for your friendship, your honesty and your continued support.

Here's to the first of many great stories together!

He's not her father's pick. But he's her only option.

Gage Barrett's goal is to bring one of the biggest crime bosses in the city to his knees. The man runs drugs, extorts money, and has the profits laundered by the pretty Angelena's father. Gage just has to get close enough to find the evidence he needs to put the guy away for good before another family is forced to live through a pain Gage is all too familiar with.

Angelena Bianco doesn't understand why her father is so insistent she marry the son of one of his clients. Santo is a thug and she wants nothing to do with him. It will be a cold day in hell before she'll walk down any aisle to that man. When the day comes for her to get married, it will be to a man of her choosing, not her father's.

Lena has two months and few options. She needs to find a husband, fast before she's forced into a situation she can't live with.

Her Choice

Chapter One

"**M**ARY SAID YOU WERE LOOKING FOR ME?" ANGELENA Bianco smiled at her father as she strolled into his study, though confusion settled in when he didn't immediately acknowledge her.

When he did raise his head, he didn't look her in the eye. "I've found you a husband."

She stopped in her tracks. "Excuse me?" Her father had *found* her a husband. She didn't realize she was looking for one. She continued forward into the room and laughed, though the sound lacked true amusement.

"It's time you married."

Laughter cut off cold, Lena stared openmouthed at her father. Where was this coming from? Her father had never pressed her to marry. Why now?

She closed her eyes, and took a deep breath. Make that two. She tried a different tactic. "Papa—"

"The deal has been made, Angelena."

Angelena Bianco dropped like dead weight into the over-stuffed wingback chair. Her father's desk, large and nicked with age, stood centered in front of the east-facing wall. The mid-morning sun streamed between the heavy paisley curtains hanging in the twin windows of her father's office, slicing the dark interior into sections. Dust mites danced in the shimmering beams, tickling her nose. As a small child, she'd been comforted by the cozy feel of the room and the smell of the books lining the shelves. She'd sit for hours

1

curled in one of the chairs while her father worked, sometimes peppering him with questions, more often simply relishing the opportunity to share the space with him.

Over the years, however, he'd changed. He smiled less, rarely laughed, and preferred the solitude of his office to spending time with his only daughter. As she grew older, they spent less time together and he answered fewer questions. When she became more curious about his business, he began working behind a locked door. These walls no longer held a sense of security, but rather a wealth of secrets.

After many foiled attempts to rebuild their relationship, she'd given up. Now they simply co-existed in the same house, sharing pleasantries and the occasional meal.

But today, not so much. Today, anger edged out every other emotion. Disbelief, a little bit of humiliation, and even a smidgeon of hurt at the insinuation she wasn't equipped to find a suitable man simmered underneath. Maybe he sympathized over the fact that she had yet to meet a man willing to commit to a future with her. It's not as if she dated scores of men looking for Mr. Right. What gave him the idea she wanted to get married in the first place? It's not like they ever talked about it.

She replayed his words in her head. "Wait a minute. The deal has been made? What is this, some kind of business arrangement?"

"In the old country—"

She threw up a hand and closed her eyes, taking another fortifying breath, and counted to ten before she opened them again to stare across her father's workspace. He watched her, the blank expression on his face not offering a hint of what was going through his head.

"We don't live in the old country, Papa. We don't do arranged marriages anymore. And I certainly won't agree to one," she stated softly. Clearly, she'd made a mistake remaining at home for so long out of concern and sympathy for her only living relative, wishing that one day they'd reestablish the father daughter relationship she yearned for.

"Well, I did grow up in the old country, as did your future father-in-law, and I've decided to choose a husband for you."

She glared at her father. "Listen, Papa—"

He shook his finger at her.

She suddenly felt five years old, being taken to task for muddying the hallway floors. Damn if that little recollection didn't leave a funny feeling in the pit of her stomach.

"You're almost thirty years old, Lena. Past time to begin your life as a wife."

She rolled her eyes. "You make it sound like a job." She was way past the age when her father could make such an important decision for her. Especially when he had no clue as to her preferences for a husband. Not that she had any. "If Mama were alive, she'd whack you with her soup spoon for such a comment." At least she hoped her mother would have. Doesn't every mother want her children to live their own lives, make their own choices, get a good education, a solid job and eventually get married? When the time was right?

"If your mother were alive she'd be nagging you for grand babies."

Lena sighed and looked down to where she'd grasped her locket, the only keepsake she had of her mother's. It held a picture of her parents on the day they married, and one with her mother holding her as a baby. "I'd like to think she'd want me to fall in love first."

Her father tsked, but a sad look came over his face and his eyes glazed over. Was he thinking about the wife he lost so long ago?

"I'm not marrying a man I don't even know, Papa."

Her father shook his head. "That won't be a problem. You do know him."

At this, her head shot up. She tried to catch her father's eyes, but he appeared to be scouring the papers spread out on his desk before him.

"Who?" A sense of foreboding slithered over her skin, raising goose bumps in its wake.

He cleared his throat and ran his finger down one of the pages he pretended to read, stopping halfway, moving that same finger across a line of print. Three times.

"Who?" she demanded, fighting not to grind her teeth together.

He licked his lips and fidgeted with his glasses, then scratched his nose. He dropped his gaze back to the papers, then over to stare at the blank computer screen. Next, he scanned the rows of books on the shelves.

Every nerve ending on Lena's body went on high alert. The hair stood on the back of her neck.

"Papa," she growled. "Look at me. Now."

He raised his head, but looked over her shoulder instead of at her. His typical technique for avoidance.

"Who, exactly, did you make this *arrangement* with?"

He swallowed. His throat moved up and down. Was that a bead of sweat on his brow?

She knew. Before he gathered his thoughts. Before he opened his mouth. She had no idea how. But she knew who her father had signed her life away to before the words could pass over his lips. Rage, disgust and bitter disappointment battled as they rushed through her system.

"Father?" she whispered. Her throat had gone dry and she couldn't bring herself to use the loving, more affectionate term of Papa. The one he used to bend to when she was a child, especially just after her mother died.

He winced, but then schooled his reaction into one of determination. "With Giovanni Soranno. His son, Santo, has asked for your hand. And I have accepted on your behalf." He nodded firmly as though that sealed the deal.

Lena gasped. For a long moment she sat dumbfounded, at a loss for words as her heart beat at a frantic pace behind her breast once it restarted after the initial shock. She almost tilted her head to see if water might drain from her ears and clear the whooshing sound.

"You can't be serious," she whispered.

When he didn't smile and tell her this was his first ever attempt at some twisted practical joke, she jumped from the chair and smacked her hands flat to his desk, hardly noticing the sting to her palms.

He jerked back.

Guilt etched his face, but she forced down the instinctive desire to mollify him.

"You had no right." She growled the words between teeth clenched tight, so angry she shook.

"Angelena—"

"Don't—" Fury roared through her. Tears swam, blurring her vision. "You had absolutely no business making such an agreement without my knowledge. None! I'm an adult, Father, not a child. I don't need my daddy picking a husband for me. I don't *want* my daddy picking a husband for me."

She spun around, giving him her back, closed her eyes and counted to ten. To twenty. To fifty. "Call it off."

"I can't."

"*Yes*, you can."

"You don't understand—"

She twirled around so fast, she felt her hair, always so snug in its clasp on her head, shift and wobble, threatening to lose its tenuous hold. "No, *you* don't understand, Papa. Santo is arrogant. He's crude. He makes me feel like a piece of meat he wants to chew on."

Santo Soranno had been sniffing around her since she'd hit puberty. When she'd finally gone off to college, it had been a reprieve from his constant sexual innuendos and advances, some more blatant than others.

She remembered when he'd cornered her after school one day during their senior year. In the empty hallway, Santo had pushed against her back, pressing her into the lockers. Then he'd skimmed his filthy hand along her torso toward her breast, slow and torturous. If it wasn't for his younger sister appearing out of nowhere, Lena had no clue what might have happened. Nothing deterred or scared him, not even back then. Other than his father. When Rosa reminded Santo their father planned to pick them up and didn't like waiting, he'd cursed and copped a quick, painful feel, then retreated.

And now, her father has apparently agreed to just hand her over to the grown up version of that boy.

A shiver rolled over her, leaving her icy cold. "Papa, Giovanni may be a client of yours, but I'm not one of his fans. And I *detest* his son."

Santo's father creeped her out. Rumors abounded he was involved in organized crime, but of course there was no solid proof to substantiate such claims. A rich man, he had many business holdings. Although he preferred not to be in the public eye, he did good things for the community. People hesitated to press the issue when he constantly gave thousands to charities and built homes for people who needed them.

But his youngest son, Santo, was a bully who had no trouble using scare tactics and threats to get what he wanted.

"He's one of my best clients, Angelena. I've known Giovanni for years. You went to school with his children. This will be a good match."

Angelena had the insane urge to giggle.

Giovanni Soranno had to be close to sixty, but he looked ten years younger. Handsome was too weak a word to describe him. He exuded charm, wore his wealth like a conservative business suit, and had impeccable manners. He laughed showing off a beautiful smile. He played the all-American man. Hell, he even encouraged his friends and business partners to call him John instead of Giovanni. Lena, though, had no use for him. That smile of his never warmed the blackness in his eyes.

Every ounce of gossip had at least a grain of truth to it. He appeared too perfect. And in her experience, nobody was perfect. However, his acting skills were stellar.

Unfortunately, every time she tried to warn her father to be more selective in the people he dealt with, he brushed her fears aside, claiming she watched too much television. He insisted Mr. Soranno was a respected businessman.

But where Giovanni was as suave and smooth as a car salesman, Santo was as disgusting and rude as a punk ass gang banger. He had his father's looks, but none of the personality. If his father was the snake, Santo was the oil.

Lena cringed, bile rising in her throat. No way in hell was she marrying that horrible man. "I will not marry him, Papa."

"Yes, Angelena, you will."

"*No*. I won't." She stifled the urge to stomp her foot like she did when she was ten and he refused her requests for a sleepover.

"I cannot break this agreement, Lena."

She returned to the chair, but leaned forward trying for a conciliatory pose, desperate to get her father to see reason. "Do you really want me married off to a man I don't love, never mind one I don't even like being in the same room with?"

"I'm sure he's not that bad. You may even learn to love him."

She gaped, struggling to find words. Swallowing, she sat back in the chair and looked across the desk at somebody she'd respected her entire life, even more so after she'd watched him pine for the love of his life since the day she'd closed her eyes and never woke up.

"Learn to love him? Papa, you don't *learn* to love some-body. Either you do or you don't. And believe me, I have absolutely no plans to love that man. *Ever.*" Kill him perhaps, if forced to spend her life with him. But love him? Not even on her deathbed.

"Lena—"

She needed to get him off this kick, and quickly.

Angelena stood and smoothed a hand down her dress, preparing to leave. "When I'm ready, I will find the man I want to spend the rest of my life with."

"The wedding will be during the long weekend in September."

"What!" How many more surprises would fall into her lap today? Considering it was not even noon yet, the day was young. "That's two months away." This was spiraling out of control faster than she could breathe.

"Santo isn't in the country at the moment, but he'll be home in plenty of time."

Her flight instinct kicked in. She shoved down the scream battling to be set free.

"We don't live in Sicily, Papa," she finally said, her voice low but not too steady. "You and Mama left there long before I was born. I'm a modern, American woman. When, and if, I fall in love, *I'll* decide if I'm going to marry him. The choice is mine to make. Not anybody else's."

"John has hired somebody to help you with all the necessary arrangements. You won't have to do a thing but look beautiful. The wedding will be at their home."

He wasn't listening to a word she said.

"Goodness, what woman could turn that down?" She huffed. "Would I at least get to pick out my own wedding dress?"

He titled his head, casting her an offended look. "Of course."

Her anger melted away, some of it. She sighed. There had to be a way to make him understand. She needed time. If Santo wasn't in town, perhaps she had some. It wasn't much, but she few options without completely disrespecting her father. "Papa, I won't marry Santo. I will only marry a man of my own choosing."

"Lena—"

"At least give me some time to find a man I *want* to marry." Any man would be better. Hell, she'd even, maybe, in a million

years, with the possibility of a quick and painless death immediately following the ceremony, consider marrying Giovanni
himself. A shiver of revulsion wormed its way up her spine.

"Angelena—"

"*Please*, Papa." Desperation consumed her. "Six months.
Give me six months."

"I don't think—"

"Surely you can give me six measly months to find a man
that I actually want to marry. If I haven't found one by then..."
Then she'd have come up with another plan. She'd run, leave
the country, go into hiding and leave her father behind if she
absolutely had to. However, the thought of not seeing him
again tore her heart in two. There had to be another way. She
just needed a little time to think.

Her father slouched in his chair and ran a hand over his
face. "You have no choice in this matter. If you don't marry
Santo, his father—"

"What, Papa? What could Giovanni possibly do if I don't
marry his son?"

Her father blanched.

Fear settled like a gigantic boulder in her gut.

Her father gulped and wiped a bead of sweat from his
forehead. He closed his eyes and took a breath. A shiver
racked his body.

His strange reaction scared the crap out of her. Could
Giovanni actually *do* something to her father? There'd never
been any hint of violence in the many rumors circulating
about him. Not one. Questionable finances, unsubstantiated
claims of course, and a few moments where she didn't like
the gleam in his eyes. But nothing that would warrant the
unease she suddenly felt.

His son was a different story altogether.

"Angelena, you will marry Santo Soranno in a ceremony at their home on the Labor Day weekend in September as planned." He stopped talking but his lips continued to move.

Lena had the distinct impression her father uttered a prayer.

Before she could try to change his mind again, a knock sounded on the den door, startling both of them. It creaked open and their housekeeper poked her head in.

"Mr. Bianco, there's a phone call for you. Would you like me to transfer it into here?"

Mary winked at Lena. She had started working for Lena's parents a few years before Lena's birth. After her mother's death, Mary had been the surrogate Lena leaned on throughout the years. Right now, she wished she were five years old again. She could use a warm hug and perhaps some cookies and milk.

"Who is it, Mary?"

"It's Mr. Soranno, sir."

The tension in the room doubled, the oxygen sucked out like a backdraft. Lena faced her father. She opened her mouth.

He raised his hand. "Yes, Mary, you can transfer the call. Just give me a couple of minutes, please."

"Certainly, sir." Mary backed out and closed the heavy wood door with a soft click.

She needed to try one more time. "And if I refuse?"

When her father looked at her, sadness filled his eyes. He sighed and leaned back in his chair, looking every one of his sixty-two years. "That's not an option, I'm afraid."

What the hell did that mean?

His desk phone rang. She once joked with her father about

his ancient telephone. He'd clarified, saying it was an antique. Her father hated cell phones, computers, and current technology. Right now, they both looked at the relic as though a serpent would slither out through the handset.

"Why don't you have Gage take you for a drive? Clear your head." He spoke to her, but stared at the black heavy-duty telephone, his brows furrowed.

She stood and took two steps toward the door.

"I'm sorry, Angelena," he said softly.

She stopped, but didn't turn. She dropped her chin to her chest, took a deep breath, and then straightened her spine as she left the room.

As soon as she cleared the threshold of the office and closed the door behind her, she sagged against the wall. She needed a plan. Something quick and decisive that would put a stop to this entire fiasco. She'd rather die than spend the rest of her life with Santo Soranno. She needed another option. There had to be another option that didn't include her slipping away in the night.

"Ms. Bianco?" Gage Barrett leaned against the wall opposite her. The man looked like he ate testosterone for breakfast. Decked out in his chauffeur's uniform, one that fit him like a glove, it appeared ready to split at the seams if he flexed the slightest bit.

Their previous driver had been old and grumpy, and lacked the necessary skills to be a driver—like a sense of direction, or the ability to see above the steering wheel. She'd been concerned for their safety every time she climbed in the vehicle, more than once insisting she drive herself so he could rest his aging eyes and trembling fingers that clearly ached with arthritis.

Gage didn't fit the image either. However, he was much easier on the eyes. He handled the car like an appendage and seemed to have an alertness that other drivers didn't. His gaze took everything in, leaving her unsettled more than once after he'd given *her* a thorough twice over.

Short dark hair, broad shoulders that could probably carry the weight of the world, narrow waist and well over six feet, he had appeared out of the blue a couple of months ago. When she'd questioned her father about it, he'd simply said their previous driver had failed his re-test and couldn't hold a license anymore. The limo company had sent Gage as the replacement.

With Gage, the only risk she worried about was the possibility of combustion—hers. One of these days, her panties would go up in smoke. He belonged on a romance cover or modeling sexy underwear, not behind a steering wheel driving a financial advisor and his daughter around town. She could even envision him on a recruitment billboard for the military, encouraging every hot-blooded woman and man to enlist.

"Hello, Gage."

"Can I take you somewhere?" His deep baritone sent prickles over her arms. The good kind. The kind of shiver only a man like him could warm up.

She needed to get out of the house for a while. Maybe an idea would come to her if she cleared her mind for a few hours. "I'd like to go for a drive, if you have no other immediate obligations."

He shrugged. "It's my job."

"Then, let's go." She pushed herself away from the wall, grabbed her purse from the hallway table, and strolled to the front door.

He reached it first and held it open for her. "After you."

She passed by him and stepped out into the sunshine, catching a whiff of his aftershave. Very sharp and edgy. It fit.

"Anywhere in particular you want to go?" he asked.

"Anywhere you want to take me, is fine." As long as it was far away from here, so she wouldn't be tempted to listen in on her father's call with her future father-in-law.

Chapter Two

GAGE KNEW EXACTLY WHERE HE'D LIKE TO TAKE MS. Angelena Bianco. Straight to the nearest king-sized bed for a night of hot, raunchy, sweaty, use-every-square-inch-of-the-mattress sex.

He'd been working for the Biancos for about two months, and since day one he'd wanted to mess up the always pristine Angelena. She had the most beautiful skin he'd ever seen. It reminded him of a paint color his mother once put on their living room wall. She'd searched high and low for the specific shade, took weeks to find it, in fact. Here he had the pleasure of looking at it each and every day—light caramel. And he loved to savor the sweetness of caramel on his tongue.

Her complexion was a perfect accompaniment to the dark hair she rarely let down, and her dancer's physique tripped him up good. For a man used to playing it cool, this woman created a heat inside his body only an icy plunge under the head of his waterfall shower head could fix.

He wanted to see those waves of luxurious dark tresses cascade down her back. Have the privilege of watching those beautiful dark eyes widen in pleasure and turn molten with lust. Maybe even taste her warm center.

But that would never happen, at least not while he worked for them. First, women like her didn't allow men in his current position into their inner sanctum, never mind their bed, unless they were looking to slum for a night, had something to prove, or somebody to piss off. Second, it violated one of his personal rules—never sleep with the target. When he was on the job, especially an undercover one, he never got involved with anyone. It was too risky. Not that she herself was the target, but close enough.

But man oh man, she sure tempted him to break the rules. "I work for you, Ms. Bianco. I go wherever you tell me to go."

She paused but her gaze flicked up to his then meandered down his body before darting back to his face. Interesting. It was the first time she'd looked at him, rather than through him.

"Call me Lena." She shoved a pair of black Gucci sunglasses over her nose and strutted out the door toward the limo.

And the conservative, uptight, beautiful, untouchable daughter of the man he worked for was back.

Gage followed behind, watching the sway of her ass with each step. Her pink linen dress hugged her slim curves. But it was the pearls around her long, slender neck that really did it for him. He envisioned them draped over her breasts with her nipples peeking through the strands. "Okay, *Lena*, are you in the mood for dining, shopping, or maybe the museum?"

"I'm not in the mood for any of those. Just blue sky and quiet. Something different from the norm would be nice."

Gage swept his arm wide, encompassing the upscale neighborhood she lived in, with the executive style homes, multi-car garages and pretentious, though beautiful, land-scaping. "You do realize we're in the middle of New York?"

"Yes, I do, Gage, which is why I expect we'll be gone for a few hours."

"Does your father know you're going out?"

She looked straight at him. Though he couldn't see her eyes through the tinted lenses, he felt the heat of her glare.

Thank you Neiman Marcus for the double-breasted suit coat currently concealing his junk, because there was nothing hotter than a pissed off female. In four inch heels she just about matched his six two. Which put her at the perfect height.

"I'm an adult, Gage. I think I can decide for myself when I go out, where I go, how long I'm gone," she swallowed and licked her lips, "or who I go with."

"I won't argue with that. Just wasn't sure if he needed me or not."

"He's working from home today and mentioned no other plans. If he needs to go out, I guess he'll have to drive himself or call a cab."

She was definitely in a snit today.

Gage turned away before she noticed his grin. "Let's go then." He opened the back door of the limo and tipped his head. "Your chariot awaits, Princess."

Gage patiently stood at attention while she settled herself on the dark gray leather seat, prim and proper, knees together, tipped to the left, and ankles crossed. Her dress hiked higher, giving him a scrumptious view of thigh and a glimpse of a blemish on her skin a couple of shades darker than her natural tone and about the size of a quarter. The beauty had a beauty mark. Interesting. Was it the only one?

"Is there anything in here to drink?"

"I have some bottled water and juice on ice."

"Anything stronger?"

Tough day. "Little early for that, wouldn't you say?" She did seem more rigid than normal, and that was saying a lot. "There's some Scotch in the decanter in the bar. Would you like me to pour you a glass?"

She shook her head. "I'll do it. Let's go." With a wave of her hand, she dismissed him.

Gage closed the door, forcing himself not to slam it harder than necessary. He strode around to the driver's side and got in. Before he started the engine, he twisted around so he could see her through the partition. "Would you like me to close this?"

"No. That's fine."

"Are you sure?"

"I'm sure I said it was fine."

Usually she simply ignored him. The fact she was speaking to him at all was a major step forward. If she was finally willing to acknowledge him, maybe he could find out just how much she knew about her father's business. Gage turned the key in the ignition, shifted into gear, and headed down the driveway.

He hung a right at the end and slowly accelerated, smoothly navigating down the street, past homes that cost far more than he could afford on his paycheck. Most of the people in this area of town had lived here for years, generations even. The trees were large and provided enough shade to darken most of the street. Some lucky landscape crew probably made a fortune keeping the extensive gardens magazine worthy. Kids didn't play in the street here. They had pools and tennis courts to keep them entertained. Though if he had to guess, the majority of the families didn't have children young enough to warrant tiny plastic play structures.

Keeping one eye on traffic, he expertly guided the limo through the narrow streets out toward the highway. Gage kept his other eye on the rear view mirror and Angelena. She'd pulled out the pins holding her hair in place, dropped her head back against the bench seat, pressed her right cheek to the cool leather, and gazed out the side window. She sighed; an exaggerated inhale and exhale of breath, making those luscious breasts of hers rise and fall. Her shallow scooped neckline didn't offer him a glimpse of the treasures she hid beneath, but he had a fantastic imagination. And right now, his mind conjured up light pink material with a faintly raised lacey pattern covering her chest area.

Normally he was an ass man, but Angelena Bianco had a gorgeous rack. A perfect handful with a little extra. Were they even real? Why women of her caliber could not leave things as God intended, he would never know. The too-perfect picture she displayed meant she probably camouflaged the flaws.

They hit the interstate and Gage picked up speed to merge into the rush of cars and transport trucks heading out of the city. With no specific destination in mind, he just settled back and drove.

When he'd volunteered for this assignment, Gage had high hopes it wouldn't take long to get close to the one he was gunning for. It had taken him years to find the man responsible for what happened to his brother, and since then, he'd been on a single-minded mission to end Giovanni Soranno's lucrative and illegal career. But the cagey bastard remained discreet in his business dealings. He had people fooled. Traits that probably kept him alive and prosperous.

Instead, two months later Gage was still searching for a way to integrate himself smack dab in the middle of the inner circle. Or to at least be a tag along with Lena's father on one of his business dealings, so he could get a lay of the land and strategize a different option. Gage preferred the quick in and out method. Liked it fast, hard, and over with as quick as possible so he could move on to the next challenge.

He attacked relationships the same way. Unfortunately, he had no clue how to catch the man he was after. The various authorities were well aware of his criminal activity, but had yet to gain any solid evidence to put him away. Giovanni Soranno conducted what appeared to be a legitimate business to the naked eye.

His oddity, however, was that he attended a limited number of public events. On those few occasions he ventured out among the riff-raff, his security detail only allowed those with gold-embossed invitations close enough to see the irises of his eyes.

As a result, the months were dragging by and Gage was losing patience. He wanted this asshole now, before another family suffered.

While Gage drove the Biancos all over the city, his partner chased down potential leads, dealt with the various recording devices they had in place, and conducted stakeouts at some of Soranno's regular haunts. So far, nothing had panned out. If they didn't find something soon, or make significant progress, their superiors would yank them out and drop another team in. Gage did not intend to let that happen.

He snuck a peek at his temporary employer's daughter to find her slouched with her legs stretched out, glasses pushed on top of her head, her fingers wrapped around an empty glass of Scotch. She chewed her bottom lip and squinted her eyes as she gazed out the window. Maybe she was hatching a plan to buy the entire summer line at Macy's, but needed to add extra closet space to her room first.

He realized she'd rolled her head back and was looking

directly at him. He averted his gaze from the look he saw in her eyes. Was that pain or anger? "Need something, Princess?" he called out, his attention back on the road in front of him.

She grimaced. "Please don't call me that."

Gage had the insane urge to trace the perfect arch of her eyebrows with the tip of his finger. Smooth out the frown lines that puckered the area between her eyes. Then press his lips to the middle of her forehead.

"Where are we going?" she asked, though her tone suggested she didn't give a rat's ass about the actual destination.

"Nowhere in particular."

She cocked her head, studying him with a narrowed gaze. "Are you married, Gage?"

He glanced at her through the rear view mirror. "Nope."

"Fiancée, girlfriend, friend with benefits?"

"Getting kind of personal aren't you?"

She shifted her gaze back to the window.

He waited for a few minutes before he responded. "No, no and no."

"Why?"

He shrugged. "Haven't found the right woman. No real interest. Besides, work tends to get in the way of establishing a relationship."

"I guess you're always on standby, waiting for your employer to need a lift somewhere, huh?"

"Yeah, something like that."

"Do you have family?" This was the chattiest she'd ever been with him. Normally she spat out clipped instructions and then ignored him.

"Doesn't everyone?"

She grunted.

"My parents live in Houston."

"Huh. You don't have an accent," she said.

"I haven't lived there in a very long time."

"Any siblings?"

"An older sister," he replied.

"Brothers?"

He paused for three full heartbeats as an image of a mini version of himself strolled through his mind. "No."

"Are you close to your family?"

At one time, they'd been his whole life. "Not anymore."

"I'm an only child," she told him. "It sucks."

Time to turn the tables. Might as well take advantage of the opportunity to gather some information. "You like selling real estate?"

"I do. I like putting people into the right homes."

"Never wanted to follow in your father's footsteps?" he asked.

"Nope. Never."

"He seems to do well as an investment banker. He must have some pretty big clients."

"I guess."

"Where's your mother?" Though he already knew the answer to that one.

"She died when I was five. I hardly remember her."

"I'm sorry."

"Yeah, me too." A tear fell from the corner of one eye and trickled down her pale cheek.

"Hey, are you okay?" Guilt flooded him.

She shook her head. Then nodded. After a harsh swipe at her face to obliterate the tears that followed, she poured another drink and gulped it down.

Crap. Guilt be damned, he had no intention of becoming entangled in some female angst. Neither did he relish the idea of chauffeuring a drunk socialite around. But he wasn't a total ass. She obviously needed time to herself. He suspected she wouldn't appreciate him witnessing her breakdown. Gage raised the partition and turned his full attention to his pretend job.

They'd gone ten miles past the city limits, every one of them passed in silence, when he lowered the partition again. She'd tidied herself up and straightened in her seat. Miss Composed was back in the game.

"I'm hungry. Are you hungry, Gage? Would you like to get something to eat with me?"

He'd like to eat her, but he couldn't say that. The fantasy of her shocked outrage at such a crude suggestion almost made him chuckle. "I could go for something."

"Great. Let's find a place to grab some food."

"If you haven't noticed, we're not in the middle of downtown New York. There's no five-star restaurants out here. No valet parking and certainly no posh eateries that qualify as a place to see and be seen."

She frowned. "Is that what you think of me? That I only eat in the most elite dining establishments?"

If the pearls fit.

"Right now, I'd really love a nice juicy burger and fries. The more grease and calories the better." She cocked her pretty head to the side and pinned him with a steely stare. "I'm sure we can find a pub or local joint somewhere with red cracked vinyl seating that uses paper-wrapped cutlery and plays music from a wall-mounted boom box."

He laughed. This was different. The opposite of the

socialite he'd been driving around the city for the past two months, taking her to art showings, theater openings, and business dinners with her father and his associates. He'd hoped one of those dinner engagements would pay out and give him a chance to get close to Soranno. No such luck. If Soranno had been in attendance at all, he had snuck in and out with nobody being the wiser.

"Let me see if I can find something on the GPS." He punched in a restaurant search and found a little hole in the wall about three miles ahead.

Ten minutes later, they turned off the highway and cruised into the parking lot of a humble diner that had seen better days. Scarred yellow paint covered the outer shell. A large neon sign indicated that they had arrived at Flo's, established in 1975 and home of the best damn burger outside of New York City.

A handful of cars littered the disintegrating parking lot. The patrons inside stared out the window as he drove past to park the limo near the end of the building, where he would have space to back out. They probably figured somebody famous was lost and needed directions.

Angelena hopped out on her own steam before Gage managed to get around back to open the door. She stood with her hands on her slim hips, glasses perched on her slender nose, checking out the joint. "Hope the food's as good as they claim." She turned and bent down, leaning into the car. As she did, her dress tightened, creating a very snug fit around her heart-shaped ass.

His cock hardened and his palms itched with the desire to cup and squeeze those delectable cheeks. He stretched out his fingers to relieve the discomfort. He wanted to feel her rear tucked into the curve of his hips, his erection rubbing the crease in her ass. All he needed to do was block her between the door and the car, shift her dress up and over her hips and he could plunge into her tight... He took a step forward. *Whoa.* Fuck. He needed to get a grip. Gage backed up and waited by the door like the professional driver he pretended to be. When she straightened, purse in hand, he closed the door and hurried after her, stepping past her to open the door to the restaurant. They stepped inside, the bell tinkling overhead, and got a blast of air conditioning in the face. Good. His body temperature could use a cold shock right about now. The smell of fryer grease hung like smog, but the sizzle of a grill and the scent of bacon had him salivating.

He scoped out the interior, spotted the entrance to the kitchen and a short hallway that probably led to the washrooms, and perhaps a back entrance. He led Lena to a booth near the kitchen and guided her onto the bench with her back to other diners, then sat across from her, keeping his back to the wall.

She grabbed the plasticized menu, read the front, flipped it over and read the back.

"What can I get you?"

Gage looked up at their server. She wore a typical diner uniform—short-sleeved pink dress with a white apron. Her nametag read Daisy. Gage waited for Lena to answer. When she looked at him over the top of the menu, he nodded.

"Oh. Um... I'll take the banquet burger, with everything, and the seasoned fries, please."

"Anything to drink?" Daisy's face was devoid of makeup, the crow's-feet around her eyes prominent. The poor woman looked as though she'd pulled a double shift.

"An iced tea, please." Lena lowered the menu and folded her hands together over it.

"And you, handsome?" Daisy's bleached blonde hair hung in a messy, sagging ponytail. It bounced a bit as she perked up and pushed out her chest. She offered him a bright smile.

Lena's gaze ping ponged between Daisy and him. She frowned.

Gage kept his focus on the woman across the table from him. "I'll have the same, thanks."

"Coming right up. If you need anything else, just yell." She ignored Lena and sauntered away, her hips swaying a little harder than necessary.

He was male, so he had to look, but somehow, her twitching backside didn't do a damn thing for him.

Lena leaned forward and narrowed her eyes. "So, tell me about yourself, Gage. What do you like to do when you're not driving me or my father all over the city?"

He scratched his neck. Why the sudden quest to discover who Gage Barrett really was? "Not much to tell. I'm a chauffeur. It's my job."

"Sounds boring."

She didn't know the half of it. But stakeouts were worse.

"What do you do for fun?"

Put assholes who like to hurt people behind bars. He shrugged and offered his best 'not-much' look.

"Come now, you must have a hobby. You're not with us all the time. You look fit, so you must do some sort of activity besides drive."

"I'm on call twenty-four seven, so I can't afford to join the gym."

"Please don't tell me you spend all your free time as a couch potato catching up on soap operas."

He couldn't help but laugh. He'd never before seen her sense of humor. "I like motorcycles. I'm building one. So I guess you can say that's my pastime."

"Really?"

He nodded. "Really."

"I'd love to see it sometime."

Did he have a look of disbelief on his face? Because this time she chuckled. Honest laughter poured from her mouth. It had a musical quality, almost like the tinkling wind chimes his grandmother used to hang off her back deck in the summer. Angelena needed to laugh more often.

"You don't strike me as a girl who's into bikes."

"You don't know what kind of girl I am."

True. Perhaps he'd been judging a book by its cover. Someone in his line of work should know better than to do that. But in his experience, most of the time, the cover was pretty bang on. "Ever been on one?"

She scoffed. "No. My father forbade me to date any boy who didn't live up to his standards while I was in school."

"You mean the bad boys?"

"I mean the boys who didn't come from a background steeped in tradition. One that included private school and chaperones." She shrugged. "But I'm an adult now, and I have different tastes than my father." She tried to throw off the comment as flip, but her shoulders were tense, as were the lines around her mouth.

"Good to know."

"How old are you, Gage?"

"Thirty-four. How old are you, Lena?"

"Didn't anybody tell you it's not polite to ask a lady her age?"

"You started this question and answer period, not me."

She grinned and her eyes lit up. Gone was the despondent woman who'd climbed into the back of the limo a couple of hours ago. This new and improved version piqued his interest immensely.

"I'm twenty-nine." She looked down at her folded hands. "Twenty-nine and single."

Was that a simple statement of fact, or was she looking for some sort of response from him? He had no clue how to respond, so he waited her out.

"Gage, can I ask you a question?"

He made a rude noise. Of course, nobody had ever called him a gentleman. "Why ask for permission now?"

She made a face he couldn't interpret. "Do you let your parents tell you what to do?"

"My parents haven't been telling me what to do for a very long time." No need to tell her why.

She opened her mouth, ready to say something and all he could picture were those luscious pink glossed lips wrapped around his cock. She closed them again. "Never mind."

Daisy appeared with their food. As she leaned over the table depositing plates, she cast him an interested look. "If you need anything else, don't be afraid to ask." She winked at him.

Lena scowled at the back of Daisy's head.

He smiled politely. "Thank you."

Daisy straightened and spun on the toes of her dirty white runners. She shot Lena a quick, condescending look over her shoulder. "Oh, you too."

"Gee thanks," Lena muttered.

Gage choked back his laughter. He hadn't been this amused in ages.

Lena slipped the white paper ring off the paper napkin-wrapped silverware. She separated each piece, eyeballed it, and then proceeded to wipe them down with the napkin, one tine at a time.

Gage waited while she separated the fries from her burger, lifted the bun, nodded with approval at the toppings, and then sprinkled salt over her French fries. Finally, she retrieved the half-empty bottle of ketchup from the end of the table and applied a small neat puddle to an empty section of her plate. She glanced up, and caught him studying her. "Problem?"

"Not at all." He had the insane inclination to mess up her perfect circle of ketchup.

She spread the napkin over her lap, and picked up one fry, holding it between her pointer finger and thumb, pinky out. She dipped it into the ketchup—just the tip—and raised it to her mouth, biting the end off and chewing thoughtfully. She nodded, and then shoved the remainder of the fry into her mouth like a chipmunk packing away a nut.

Using two hands, she picked up the burger and checked it out from all angles. Then she opened wide enough that he got an excellent view of her sparkling white, perfectly straight teeth. She paused before claiming that first mouthful of beef and bun, blinked and looked straight at him. Her gaze dropped to his untouched food and back up again. "Aren't you going to eat?"

"Watching you is more fun." In truth, he hadn't had this much fun in a very long time.

She blushed and her olive skin darkened to an even more beautiful shade.

"I like how you treat a burger in a diner with as much class as you would an expensive steak in a five-star restaurant. Though I have to admit, I can't wait to watch you inhale that thing. See the juice dribble down your chin. Watch your eyes widen as you take pleasure in each swallow."

Her eyes grew rounder as each statement fell from his lips. Curious. Would she have the same reaction during sex?

Chapter Three

LENA'S HEART STUTTERED WITHIN HER CHEST. SHOULD she continue eating her food or drop the delicious looking burger to her plate, reach across the table and yank him by the lapels over to her side of the booth? He looked and spoke like a walking sex god, who lived and breathed the act. She rubbed her thighs together, seeking relief. No other man did that to her. No other man made her wet and needy from sexual innuendos and heated looks alone.

Since her father had introduced her to their new chauffeur, she'd been dreaming up places to go, just so she could look at him. She'd shamelessly ogled him from the back of the limo for weeks now. She actually despised going to all those museums and art galleries. What was the point of standing in front of a painting that looked like a four-year old had a tantrum with mom and dad's new color choices for the living room? She had no interest in discussing the merits of the artist's intellect, emotional capacity, and philosophy on life when the artist obviously sneezed blobs of paint on the canvas and swiped a brush through it as he leaned over reaching for a tissue.

In her experience, theaters were loaded to the rafters with pretentious snobs, and many of the restaurants where she dined were stuffy and overpriced for the child-sized portions they gave you. She'd take a perfectly done burger with a big garlic-laced slice of dill pickle and a slab of bacon any day. Throw in a side of hot, seasoned French fries, and she'd think she'd died and gone to heaven.

She did enjoy a perfectly chilled white chardonnay, though.

Did Gage like wine, or was he a beer guy through and through? She pictured him casual and outdoorsy, sitting around a campfire, tossing back a few cold lagers. Or taking charge of the grill as he cooked a couple of decent steaks. She could imagine him out on the road, riding his motorcycle, the wind in his face, the miles speeding by under two tires.

She'd never gone camping, never been to a barbeque, and certainly never rode on the back of a motorcycle. Mary purchased only the best cuts of beef. Lena lowered the burger—didn't let go of it—simply removed it from such proximity to her mouth. The scent of bacon had her salivating.

"Don't stop on my account." He smiled the most devastating, panty-melting grin. "I like watching a girl who likes her food."

Well, she did like her food. "I...ah...haven't had a hamburger in a while."

"Then go ahead, sweetheart, enjoy."

The endearment sent a funny tingle of warmth through her. Not sure if he was still making fun of her or not, she decided screw it, and dug her teeth into her lunch, taking a large bite. And almost toppled over.

Oh dear God. She *had* died and gone to heaven's burger house.

"I'm guessing by the dreamy expression on your face and the utterly orgasmic sound you just made, the food's good."

She chewed and swallowed. "Better than sex." She dabbed the corner of her mouth with her napkin.

Gage raised his beautifully shaped brows. "If that's what

you really think, then you've been having sex with the wrong men."

That could be, since she wasn't having sex with any man at the moment, and hadn't for some time. Worse, if her father and Giovanni had their way, she'd spend the rest of her life with a man she despised.

Great. Her train of thought ruined her appetite. What a waste. She shoved thoughts of the Sorannos out of her head and focused on the man sitting across from her. Now, this man, she could picture touching her. She could easily imagine his fingers trailing over her, body, a feather-light caress as they whispered over a hard nipple, down the slope of her smooth breasts, teasing her less than perfect stomach muscles before dipping into her belly button and then continuing down.

"You're blushing again, Ms. Bianco."

She darted a glance at his amused face. "I'm not used to somebody as…outspoken…as you are."

"I'll try to rein it in."

"Please, not on my account."

"Oh, I'd love to do it on your account, Ms. Bianco. At least then you'd know the difference between a good orgasm and a piece of meat."

She choked and swallowed the urge to groan as desire flowed through her, and instead rolled her eyes.

He laughed. He had a nice laugh. He always looked so stern and preoccupied while driving.

She dragged her gaze away from his. It would be a shame to ignore this delicious looking food. When he finally picked up his own hamburger and took a bite, she did the same.

They ate in a comfortable silence. A handful of people left

the establishment and a few more came in. The clamoring in the kitchen, the servers yelling their orders through the kitchen window and muted country music drifting through the ceiling-mounted speakers, filled the void.

Lena finally pushed her plate away from the edge of the table when only one morsel of the burger and a couple of fries remained.

"You're not going to finish that?"

"I'm stuffed."

"But it's only a few bites."

"I've hit my limit. I'm about to burst." She rubbed her stomach, surprised her dress hadn't split at the seams. Taking a sip of her drink, she glanced around the room. She hoped their waitress was on a break and would not be back to flirt with Gage before they left. She'd practically needed to yank on Daisy's greasy ponytail to grab her attention.

Lena's phone rang inside her purse. She retrieved it but didn't recognize the number. "Excuse me," she told Gage. "Hello?"

"Hello, Ms. Bianco?"

"Yes, who's this?"

"I'm Sonia. Mr. Soranno hired me to—"

Lena cut off the call. At Gage's questioning look, she shrugged. "Wrong number."

Since her mother's death, Lena had lived a sheltered life under her father's thumb. She respected and loved him dearly, so rarely rebelled against any rules he'd established. She'd even delayed moving out of the house so he wouldn't be lonely.

But that didn't mean she agreed with every one of his decisions. She had never outright defied her father before, but she had no intention whatsoever of marrying Santo. Which meant she had less than eight weeks to figure a way out of this ridiculous situation.

Lena glanced around the room. A young couple sat opposite each other holding hands across the tabletop while they shared a plate of pie, looking deep into each other's eyes.

Wait a minute. An insane idea popped into her head and circled for a few seconds. She tapped the tip of one finger against her mouth. It might be extreme but the situation called for drastic measures.

Looking at that other couple, she let the idea take shape. Could it work? She didn't have many options. She could leave the country, but that meant leaving her father behind. She could just not show up, but that would only delay the inevitable. Besides, she suspected Giovanni and Santo would drag her to the alter kicking and screaming if necessary.

But, what if she was already married?

That was it. A fake marriage. Okay, the marriage would need to be legitimate, but it only needed to last long enough to show the Sorannos she wasn't available. She'd worry about the next steps after Santo was long gone from the picture. If she were married to somebody else, Santo wouldn't be able to marry her. She'd need to find a husband though. Fast. Because she'd rather be lying next to her mother six feet under in cold, bug-infested soil than married to a man like Santo Soranno.

There wasn't a lot of time. Thankfully, she wasn't looking for love. Surely, she could find a man she liked well enough that she could fake it for a few months. Of course, she had to persuade him to walk down the aisle with her.

She wanted to drop her head to the table. How in the

world would she ever find a man willing to do this? Her father wasn't stupid. Neither was Giovanni. The man she chose would have to be convincing. It would have to appear to everyone that the two of them were madly in love.

And that it all happened in the span of a few short weeks.

Unfortunately, Lena didn't have time to scout potential pretend life partners in bars. Trying to find somebody online was just plain idiotic. The very thought of hitting the dating scene, testing out one guy after another until she found one interesting enough and willing to say yes, gave her hives.

Nope, she needed to choose a man now.

For the hell of it, Lena checked out all the men in sight, conducting an environmental scan of sorts. The pickings were slim. The young one in the corner was just a kid. The one over by the door was old enough to be her grandfather, and the two men in booths along the wall, appeared to be taken. A man at a table, watching her over his cup of coffee, was in dire need of a shave and a shower. A very long shower.

She swiveled in her seat, angling her head to see the counter where a few single men, probably long-distance truckers, ate their meals and chatted up the servers. Nope. Never home. She laid her eyes on the cook currently placing the next prepared meal on the pass through to the kitchen. He just didn't look happy, and she worried those might be prison tattoos on his biceps.

Discouraged, she shifted and slumped in her seat. Her gaze settled on Gage. She studied him while thinking about the type of man her father would approve of. He expected her to marry somebody sitting solidly within their social circle. A man familiar with the lifestyle she'd grown accustomed to. Preferably Italian. Most certainly Catholic. Lena cocked her head as she stuffed a fry in her mouth and chewed thought-fully. "Are you Catholic?"

"Ah, no. Why?"

She shrugged. "Just asking. Where's your family from?"

"Houston. I already told you that."

"No, I mean are you Scottish, Italian maybe?"

"Irish."

Damn. Well, they both started with the letter 'I'. That had to count for something.

She hardly remembered her mother, but she did recall her father sitting by her Mama's bed day and night until that horrible morning she didn't wake up. After that, he withdrew from everything but work. Work consumed him. On the rare occasions he spent true quality time with her, a father playing with his little girl, he promised her he'd find her the perfect husband. Being so young and eager for her father's attention, she'd always responded with, "As long as he's just like you, Papa."

Somebody like Gage was not the first choice her father would want for her. He definitely wasn't from 'the old country.' He was large and muscular, working class, maybe had a limited education, a little rough around the edges and he drove a motorcycle. She'd bet in a fight he'd come away bruised and bleeding, but he'd be the victor.

Gage reached over and touched her hand.

Lena jumped. The electricity in his touch startled her, sending tingles of awareness racing through her body like there was a party to get to. Other than all the things her father wouldn't like about him, he was perfect for her.

Time was of the essence. At least she wouldn't have to fake the desire he stoked. Maybe they'd actually learn to like each other, even become friends. They'd probably have a good laugh over it someday.

Whatever happened, she couldn't let her father discover her plan. The big question was would Gage agree to be her partner in matrimony? Would he be willing to stay married to her long enough to convince her father that she deserved a man of her own choosing and not some guy offered up on a platter through a business deal?

"So tell me, what kind of woman does Gage Barrett find attractive?"

He stopped mid-bite and stared at her as if trying to figure out a puzzle. "You ask the strangest questions."

Lena shrugged. "Curious. You said there's no Mrs. Barrett or any almost Mrs. Barrett in the picture. You said you're not even seeing anyone. So, I'm wondering, what does it take to catch your eye?" So she could make a list.

"You applying for the job?" His mouth curled into a sexy smirk. His eyes glittered with humor.

Yes, pretty much.

He finished his meal, leaving her waiting for his response before taking a deep breath. He crossed his arms, making his biceps bulge, the sleeves of his suit coat strangling them.

Her mouth dry, she reached for her drink and gulped. She placed her empty glass on the table in front of her and wrapped her hands around it, the condensation soaking her palms. "Every woman wants to know," she tossed back at him and hoped Daisy wasn't within earshot.

"Well, let's see. She has to have a good sense of humor. She has to be able to laugh at herself. She can't be a snob. I'd like to think she likes the same things that I do, or at least have an interest in trying them out. She can't be scared of motorcycles, and must be willing to get a little dirty when it's called for." He winked at her, a devilish grin tipping the corners of his lips. "Oh, and of course she's got to have big tits and a tight ass."

Lena felt like sliding under the table. She glanced down at her B-cup chest and felt the cellulite congealing in her rear end. She knew he considered her a spoiled rich girl. She did have the capacity to laugh at herself. However, lately nothing seemed that funny.

Chapter Four

"**D**ID YOU TELL YOUR BEAUTIFUL DAUGHTER THE GOOD news, my friend?" Giovanni leaned back in his chair, feet up on his polished desk, cigar clasped in his thick fingers, as he waited for Vincent Bianco's answer. The lengthy pause irritated the hell out of him. He preferred immediate responses from the people who worked for him.

No exceptions.

Even though Vincent couldn't see him, Giovanni narrowed his eyes and lowered his voice to a smoothness others envied, knowing the deadly tone would have the other man pissing himself. "Vincent. I asked you a question."

"Yes, Mr. Soranno. I told Angelena about the arrangement."

"And her response?"

Vincent paused a second time.

Giovanni heard him swallow.

"She...ah...she wasn't exactly thrilled."

"Why not?" he demanded. "Marrying my son means she'll never want for anything." As long as she stayed in line, kept her legs open and her eyes, ears, and mouth closed. However, knowing Santo, the tiniest thing would be construed as stepping off that wire-thin line. They'd have to ensure her freedom remained limited. Wouldn't want her to see or overhear something she shouldn't. Having to deal with a distraught father over his daughter's early demise tended to affect business affairs.

Unfortunately, he needed his younger son distracted. The

boy had no discipline and too much rage—a virtual time bomb—the complete opposite of his older brother. Vincent's daughter would keep the kid occupied for a while. At least until he could make sure his oldest son was deeply seated in the business and prepared to take over when the time came. After all, a man had to look out for his legacy. And a father had to look out for his favorite child.

When Santo spotted her a few months back at some event she'd been at with her father, he'd bitched about not getting between the pristine Angelena's legs when he'd been a randy teenager. Apparently, Vincent's daughter weighed heavily on his son's conscious. Giovanni had finally had enough and told him to marry the woman. Then he could get between her legs as often as he liked.

"She...ah...she wants to find her own husband, sir."

"What does she know?" he scoffed. "She's just a woman." A beautiful one, but still a piece of ass with legs. He adjusted his pants. If his son couldn't keep her happy, perhaps he should step in and show the boy how it was done.

"Mr. Soranno, sir, I'm not sure my daughter is the right woman for your son. Perhaps you could rethink—"

"I'm not rethinking anything, Vincent. We had a deal. You promised to repay when the time was right. Santo wants your daughter. End of discussion." He lowered his voice further, making the threat clear to his investment manager. "And you know what will happen if he doesn't have her, don't you?"

"Y- Yes, sir. I understand."

Vincent may be a spineless fool, which made him easy as hell to manipulate, but he was a genius with money. When the opportunity had fallen into Giovanni's lap years ago, he'd had no idea when and how he'd call up the loan. His gut had only told him then that it would pay off. And it had. In millions. He'd even managed to keep the financial wizard at bay by not allowing him to repay the loan until he'd decided the time was right. Nor did he tell him the delay added interest. Interest that couldn't be paid in the form of cold hard cash.

"Good. Now, on to other business," Giovanni tapped his gold plated pen on his desk. "Change of plans. I need to see you tonight." Tomorrow he had other appointments that he could no longer put off. He rubbed the constant ache in his right temple.

"But I'd hoped—"

"Hoped what?" he asked. Not that he cared.

"Nothing, sir. What time would you like to meet?"

"Nine o'clock at your office."

"Yes, sir. I'll have my driver drop me off and I'll be waiting by the back entrance at ten minutes before the hour."

"Good. I won't have time to have your office checked out in advance, so this will be a quick conversation. Now. One more thing before I go. I've arranged for the wedding planner to contact your daughter. Everything will be taken care of. She won't have to worry about a thing."

"I would think Angelena would like to help with the plans for her own wedding. Maybe that will help sway her mind."

"Your daughter doesn't have a choice in the arrangements, Vincent."

Giovanni envisioned the man's head hanging, his right hand rubbing his own temple, but from frustration, not pain. Giovanni owned this man, like he did every man who worked for him. However, every now and then he felt the need to send a little reminder.

"Your beautiful daughter is lucky she's being given until Labor Day, Vincent. Remember that. If I decided it to be so, this arrangement could be taken care of by the end of the week. The only reason for the delay is that Santo wanted to spend a few months in Sicily."

His son had used the excuse that he needed time to sow his oats. Not that he wouldn't continue sowing them after the wedding. Giovanni just hoped he stayed engaged with his new wife long enough to stay out of trouble. "Your job, Vincent, is to make sure the pretty Angelena gets used to the idea that she will become Mrs. Santo Soranno."

"Yes, sir. I will." Defeat poured from Vincent's words.

"Make sure you do. Because, Vincent…" He paused, lengthening the moment just the right amount. "If your daughter decides not to go through with this marriage, well, then I guess she'll be planning a funeral." He chuckled. "Oh. Wait. She wouldn't be around to plan one, would she?"

Dead silence on the other end, but Giovanni knew he still held Vincent's attention. "I really don't want to look for a new investment banker, Vincent. After all the years we've worked together, you know me well. I trust you with my money. I'm too old to start over again. *Abbiamo una comprensione?*"

"Yes. I understand, Mr. Soranno. My daughter will be happy to be married to your son, sir."

Well, Giovanni wasn't so sure about that, but at least there'd be a ring on her finger and his son wouldn't be making noise about wanting an office at the end of the hall, or trying to make changes to how the business was run.

A knock sounded on his office door. He glared across the room. His staff knew when faced with a closed door, they stayed the fuck out.

"I'll see you later tonight, Vincent." He hung up. "What?" he yelled as his feet hit the floor with a hard thud.

The heavy wood door swung open and a bottled redhead poked her pretty face around the edge. "Giovanni, sweetie, are you coming back to bed?"

"I told you to call me John," he growled. He was only Giovanni in the old country and to his immediate family. In America, dealing with American business people, he preferred John. He'd near perfected the dialect to go along with the image. Only when he was agitated, could a person detect his accent. Of course, when rage overtook him, he actually slipped into Italian.

"But Giovanni is sooo sexy." The whore purred, pouting her collagen filled lips.

His dick stirred. "Get your ass in here and close the door. Lock it. Then get over here and do what you do best." He undid his pants and pulled out his flaccid cock while she did as told. She hurried over to the desk and dropped to her knees. He gripped her hair and yanked hard, ignoring her yelp as he shoved her face into his crotch.

Apparently, she needed a little reminder today, too.

Chapter Five

SHE WASN'T EXACTLY LIVING UP TO THE PICTURE HE'D painted of her. She displayed proper manners, had this haute couture look and feel about her. But vulnerability hid beneath a boatload of determination. He couldn't stop himself from opening his mouth and saying shit just to push her buttons.

When his phone vibrated in his pocket, Gage pulled it out. "Barrett."

"Hello Gage. I have an unexpected meeting at the office tonight at nine. I'll need you to pick me up." Vincent Bianco's voice sounded strained on the other end of the line.

"Of course, sir." Gage checked the time on his watch. "I'll be at your front door by eight fifteen." Gage disconnected and put the phone back in his pocket. "Time to go."

She straightened in her seat. "I thought you worked for me."

"Technically, I work for your father." He raised his hand to signal Daisy for the check. "Only you by extension."

She snorted her displeasure.

"Your father has a meeting tonight that he needs me to take him to."

She drew her shoulders back as her eyes darkened and her lips thinned. "I'm sure he does," she muttered under her breath.

Gage had good hearing and caught every syllable. Now *she* seemed stressed.

Lena grabbed her purse, dug inside, and pulled out a stylish wallet.

"Let me get it." He reached into his back pocket for his own wallet.

Her head jerked up. "I'll pay for my own meal."

"Look it's no—"

"I said I'd pay," she said through clenched teeth, but then she closed her eyes and took a deep breath. When she opened them again, the quick to rise anger had dimmed and she'd unlocked her jaw. "I'm the one who asked you to find this place. I'll pay for my own food." She dipped her pretty head. "But thank you."

He held his hands up in mock surrender. "Suit yourself."

She dropped a twenty on the Formica, enough to cover her food plus a tip. He added his own cash to the pile, rose from his side of the table and waited until she did the same. Then he followed her out the diner's door and back to the limo.

She hesitated at the car, and looked back over her shoulder. Would Miss I-can-do-it-myself open her own door? He slowed his steps. She harrumphed and reached forward, but at the last second, he beat her to it, opened the door and winked at her as he did. The scowl on her face softened and he detected a near chuckle as she climbed inside and settled on the plush leather bench seat.

"Is there anything I can get you before we head back to the city?" From this angle, he had a decent view of her cleavage and the flutter of her pulse in her neck.

She peered up at him from beneath thick, black lashes. "No. I'm fine. Thank you."

He nodded and enclosed her in the car, hesitating a moment before stepping around the rear of the vehicle. He sucked in some not-so fresh country air. He needed a drink. A double. Too fucking bad he'd be on duty for a few more hours yet.

Gage took his seat up front. The moment he started the engine, she raised the privacy glass. Guess she wasn't into after-dinner conversation. Fine by him. Just proved that her moment of lowering herself to get to know the staff was simply that, a moment. Now she was back to her true self. Sadly, that left him feeling a little put out.

After a silent drive back into town, Gage pulled up in front of her family home and hopped out. This time, she waited for him to open the door like a good little rich girl. He hung back when she started up the front stairs. She met her father on his way down. Gage paced around the car, pretending he was looking at the cleaning job he'd have to do after the long drive.

"Papa. You're heading into the office this late?"

"Yes, Lena. I have a meeting."

"With who?"

Her father glanced away and tried to step around her, but she blocked him. "Father. Who?"

"Lena, it's work. Nothing more." The older man kissed his daughter on the forehead. When she didn't react, he stepped around her and continued down the stairs to the car, looking resigned. "I don't plan to be late."

"Are you meeting with Mr. Soranno?" Her tone contained more than a hint of anger. It contained an accusation.

Gage's ears perked up.

"Feel free to tell him I have no plans to go through with it, Papa."

"Angelena—"

No plans to go through with what?

"*Never.* You would have to drag me kicking and screaming." She raced up the remaining stairs, entered the house, and slammed the door behind her.

What was she talking about? Did Soranno want her to do a job for him? Was she as crooked as her father? The idea of Angelena lowering herself to the standards of a man like Giovanni Soranno rocked Gage back on his heels. The intel they'd gathered so far indicated the daughter wasn't involved in any illegal activity. Didn't mean she hadn't simply been extra careful.

Vincent sighed heavily, looking like he carried the weight of the world on his stooped shoulders. Well, at least the weight of Giovanni's world. What was Lena refusing to do?

Vincent stopped when he reached the car. "You can drop me off at the office, Gage. I'll call you when I'm ready for you to pick me up."

"Yes, sir." Gage opened the door and waited while his employer climbed in.

With Vincent in the back and the privacy partition still in place, Gage slid his cell phone out from his pocket and sent a quick coded text message to his partner, letting him know the plan for the evening.

Wade would get in place, ready to keep his eyes open and stay alert after Gage drove away. Vincent always waited for him to leave, as though he didn't want to be caught doing something, like maybe meeting with one of the city's biggest crime bosses.

Gage put the limo into drive and pulled away from the house, his mind still partially on his impromptu outing with Angelena as he turned back onto the street and then maneuvered through traffic, this time in the opposite direction, heading downtown to Vincent's office.

The normally elusive and quiet daughter of Giovanni's money launderer could hardly be described as a talkative peach, but today was unusual even for her. Something had been on her mind when she'd first climbed into the limo, and then again on the drive home. Maybe she'd been thinking about this thing she refused to do for her father. Something he'd give a year's salary to know.

Until now, he and Wade had focused on getting to Soranno through Vincent, but perhaps his daughter was the key.

They made it downtown in less than forty minutes. Gage pulled up in front of Vincent's building, a large, modern high rise in the middle of the financial district. Smoked glass panels covered the front of the gray building. Bianco's company resided on the top floor of the twenty-story structure. Gage left the car idling while he got out and opened his passenger's door.

"I'll give you a call when I'm ready to head home," Vincent said.

"Yes, sir."

Without another word, his employer stepped back from the curb. Watching in the rear view mirror, Gage saw Vincent walk toward the main entrance and even pull out his key ring, as though he planned to stroll straight inside. With a quick, over the shoulder glance in both directions, he changed course and hurried to the corner of the building, then ducked into the alley. Presumably, he assumed Gage was far enough away not to notice.

Gage noticed everything. And he wasn't worried. His partner Wade would be back in the alley, hiding and watching.

Gage pulled over a couple of blocks down and shut the car off. He waited for word from Wade. Every inch of him wanted to hop from the vehicle and run back, but they couldn't risk Vincent seeing him.

These late day meetings always played out the same way. Gage would drop Vincent off a few minutes before the hour and then drive off as though he planned to waste the time waiting in the nearest coffee shop until the boss called for a pick up. With any luck, tonight would be the night Soranno would show his face on one of the cameras they'd rigged in the alley. An even better score would be recording a conversation they could use during the trial. And if all the stars were aligned and he found a horseshoe up his ass, they'd actually catch the two men in the middle of an exchange.

Gage wasn't holding his breath. They'd had no such luck to date, or *any* luck, for that matter.

Gage drummed his fingers on the steering wheel, his gaze locked on the rear view mirror. Damn, but they needed to catch a break soon.

Cars passed. A couple of city buses passed. People strolled by, a few taking glimpses in the limo, trying to see through the tinted windows, scurrying away when they realized he was sitting in the car.

His phone buzzed once then fell silent. He didn't bother looking. It was Wade's signal he was on his way. He set watch on the side mirror.

Finally, his partner sauntered up the sidewalk, looking as though he didn't have a care in the world. A man out for the evening, perhaps on his way to meet his date for a late dinner. Gage disengaged the door locks.

Wade opened the passenger door, climbed in and slammed

it shut behind him. He shifted in his seat, his back to the glass, his gaze straight at Gage. "Nothing."

Gage smacked the steering wheel. Hard. "Fuck."

Giovanni was deep into running drugs and extortion as well as money laundering. Soranno took the money he made and had it cleaned through Vincent Bianco before he bought more narcotics to push on kids too young to understand the ramifications of their actions.

More recently, they'd been hearing through the grapevine that Soranno had branched out into the ecstasy market, which meant he wasn't content with selling on street corners, now he planned to hit the party scene as well.

"Soranno didn't even get out of the car. I have to hand it to the guy. He knows how to keep a low profile. Any luck with the phone taps?" Wade asked.

"Not from the office phones. Vincent must be using his home phone for calls with Soranno. But I haven't been able to get into his office at the house to set up the tap."

"That's the only thing that makes sense. We need to get eyes and ears in the office and the conference room here, so we can at least overhear Vincent's end of the conversation, in case he changes tactics. You need to get inside his study."

Wade nodded. "I'll work on that. I'm stopping at the precinct tomorrow to give the captain a status update. I'll make the arrangements then."

"What about the cameras on his floor of the building or the ones in the alley?" Gage asked.

"Nope. The building cameras aren't working. At least not on a consistent basis."

Which meant somebody in the building's security office was on Soranno's payroll.

"The last time I tried to play drunk and snap a picture, the driver didn't let me within ten feet of the car."

"Try again. We'll need confirmation he's in the car if we can get their conversation on tape." Hell, they just needed something to guarantee them a search warrant. Right now, Gage didn't care if it covered Soranno's home, his offices or his vehicles. He just wanted something to break.

"I'll do my best. But if that guy beats the crap out of me, it's on you."

Gage snorted. "I'm sure you'll hold your own." Wade was a black belt and had been top of their class during training at the policy academy. He might come away with a fat lip or a black eye, but the other guy always fared much worse. "Bianco?"

"Looked like he was having a nice chat with a friend who was sitting in the car. The window came down about four inches. Bianco didn't even step within two feet of the car, and nothing was handed out or in through the open window." His friend sighed. "We've got fuck all. Again."

Gage closed his eyes and let his head fall back against the backrest with a muffled thump. Damn it. What was their next move? There was only one reason for a man like Soranno to be so tightly linked to a man like Vincent Bianco—to clean dirty money and then make it disappear. Giovanni didn't keep his money in US banks. He tended to hoard cash and have Vincent manage it. If they could search Vincent's office, they'd find the evidence they needed to nail the bastard. They just needed something to justify a warrant.

"Where were you earlier?"

He opened his eyes, turning his head so he could see his partner. "When?"

54

"I tried calling you this afternoon. I don't know, around three maybe. You didn't answer."

He was with Lena having a burger. Watching the juice dribble from her mouth and listening to the sexy moans she'd made with each bite. "I took Vincent's daughter for a drive."

Wade's eyebrows rose about an inch.

"What?"

"You just drove around?"

"She said she needed space so I took her out of town, and then we stopped for a bite to eat."

"Like a date?"

Was Wade teasing him or questioning him? "No. Like she was hungry and asked me to stop for food."

"Ms. Bianco prefers five-star restaurants."

Apparently, she also likes roadside diners.

Gage focused on his friend's face. They'd hit it off from the start, taking turns doing the undercover gig and hanging out during off hours. They were about the same age, both single, and both loved their work. He was the one person Gage felt comfortable enough to be himself with. Almost. Some things you don't tell even your best friend. Like the fact that this woman could tempt him to ignore one of his personal rules. Wade frowned and Gage could practically smell smoke as the gears turned.

"You look deep in thought. What's going through your head?" Whatever it was, Gage had a feeling he wasn't going to like it.

"Maybe that's our in."

"What is?" Gage asked, though he knew exactly what his partner was suggesting.

ANNE LANGE

"The daughter. You can cozy up to the daughter and we can find out if she knows anything," Wade said.

"You know I don't do that." He'd prefer to get to know Angelena Bianco for other reasons. Legitimate reasons.

He'd been on this assignment for over a year, mostly doing a shitload of research and following trails that led nowhere. Except for those that she travelled. Everything he'd learned about Angelena intrigued him. She was beautiful and so put together he felt the need to dirty her up a little. See if she was as perfect behind the mask as she wanted people to believe. She was also intelligent. He liked women with a brain. That also meant she had to know what her father was up to.

Sex for the sake of sex and then moving on, he could do. Sex for the purpose of uncovering information? Innocent people got hurt in those types of situations. Surprisingly, wanted Angelena to be innocent.

"She's got to know something," Wade continued. "She's at most business functions with her old man. Other than a couple of friends, she doesn't appear to have a love interest. Besides a couple of domestic staff and you, there's nobody else in that house. He doesn't have a wife or a lover to confide in. His daughter has to know what he's involved in. Maybe we can put some pressure on her. If she's involved, we can take them both down along with Soranno."

That got Gage's back up. Their goal was to bring Soranno's organization down, and that included Lena's father. Did it include her as well? Funny, but when he pictured her in handcuffs, it wasn't with the intent to arrest her.

Wade pulled out a cigarette.

"Not in the car, man."

Wade tucked the unlit stick behind his ear. "Don't worry.

It's for the walk back to my car." He made to leave. "Listen, think about the daughter angle. I think it might work. If her father thinks she's in danger, then maybe he'll roll on Soranno. It's a win-win situation."

Maybe. Maybe not. Did he care? Should he care? In his experience, women were looking for long-term commitments. After this job, he'd go on to the next. He didn't have time for a commitment to anything other than his job. So why couldn't he simply dismiss the fact that this woman got to him? Gage didn't know which category Lena fell into yet, but the mere idea of using her left him with a sour feeling in the pit of his stomach.

"I'll think about it. In the meantime, check the cameras at the other locations we know Giovanni and his men frequent and see if anything's turned up when we weren't looking. And do what you can to get someone inside Vincent's office in the next day or so."

"Will do. Later." Wade climbed out of the car and strolled back the way he'd come.

Just as his friend turned the corner, Gage's cell buzzed. He answered. "Yes, sir."

"I'll be ready to leave in ten minutes." Vincent's simple statement gave nothing away.

"Then I'll be there in eight minutes, sir." Gage ended the call and started the engine.

As he drove around the block, an image of Angelena Bianco jumped into his brain. One of her bound with his cuffs. But he wasn't loading her into a squad car. She was naked and kneeling at his feet.

Chapter Six

LENA STROLLED THROUGH HER EMPTY HOME, A WEIRD sense of unease niggling at her. These days the house seemed vacant and lonely. When she'd been a little girl, the expansive size offered plenty of space to run and play. Now it simply seemed desolate. She'd asked her father a number of times over the years why they didn't move, but his answer had always been the same. Her mother had loved this house.

She sighed as she passed his study and paused in the doorway. Only this morning he'd dropped his marriage bombshell on her. He probably assumed she'd obediently go along with his plan. She knew he loved her, but he wasn't a man to be extravagant or superfluous in showing affection. That should have been her mother's role. However, her mother was only a faint memory prompted by photographic reminders.

Sometimes at night, a faint recollection of them curled up together to play a board game before dinner would wander into her dreams. Mostly, Lena remembered the final days before her mother's death, when she'd looked so pale and shaky. Too tired to eat a meal with them or read her a bedtime story. She'd never admit it to her father, but she hated him for taking her mother away for those weeks before that last one. Her parents had gone on some sort of vacation, but when they'd come home, her Mama had been too ill to play with her. She'd hardly even spoken to her. Then she was gone.

Not a hands on parent, her father never took her to Disney World, or on any vacation. The trips they'd taken always included business. He didn't attend sporting events, school plays or dance recitals. He hadn't even made an appearance at her high school graduation.

He'd been apologetic afterward, said an important business meeting had kept him away. Important business meetings had always kept him away. To avoid disappointment, she'd simply stopped announcing special events or milestones in her life. She couldn't fault him for not showing up if he didn't know he was supposed to be there in the first place. Even when she'd been ill as a child, it was the housekeeper who cared for her. Not her father.

Good grades and limited friendships meant there was nothing to attract his attention. Except for the first boy she brought home, though he hadn't said anything at the time. The boy, a friend from school, had agreed to help her study for a history test. Her father didn't approve of him on sight, and later laid out his rules for dating. There would be none until she completed high school. And then he expected boys from a specific family background and without a rowdy reputation.

Her father recognized two events each year, days where he paid special, though limited, attention to her: her birthday and Christmas Day. Probably because Mary always marked the days on his desk calendar. He would take Lena out to dinner and he'd buy her a small gift. Then he went back to work. Doing whatever it was an investment banker did had kept him away from his only child for her entire life. But he was her only family and she wasn't prepared to give up on him.

He'd been working with Giovanni for years, since shortly after her mother died. On occasion, he'd taken her to an important gala, more for appearances than because he truly wanted her there. At those events, she'd watched Mr. Soranno's cold, contemplative gaze follow them around the room. Her father had always insisted she not leave his side, other than when he needed to actually speak to Mr. Soranno. Then he instructed her to powder her nose or get a drink.

And now he wanted to hand her over to the entire Soranno family.

Lena left her father's study and crossed the hallway to the family room just as the phone rang. She paused to answer it. "Hello, you've reached the Bianco residence."

"Is this Angelena?" His low and creepy voice instantly took her back to her high school days.

"Who's asking, please?" A shiver raced up her spine. All the hairs on the back of her neck rose.

"The man of your dreams, baby. It won't be long now and I'll finally have you. All of you. You were meant to be mine, you know."

"Who is this?" she demanded, wanting Santo to confirm his identity. The years had aged his voice, but the underlying threat in every word he uttered hadn't changed. He could say hello with evil intent.

"I'll be home soon, sugar. I'll be in touch as often as possible until then. Wouldn't want you to forget about me."

The line went dead. She replaced the telephone receiver and stumbled over to settle into a corner of the sofa, curling into a protective ball.

She'd been waiting about an hour, staring out the window when the front door opened. She jumped up and hurried to the foyer.

Gage Barrett stood just inside the door.

Her father strode past her with barely a glance. "Angelena dear, please get Gage a drink of water. He was having a bit of a coughing fit."

"Sure." Should she tell her father? Would Santo's call change his mind?

Gage appeared quite fine as he looked her over, the hungry look in his eyes sending her back a step or two.

She dragged her gaze away from Gage. "Papa. Do you have time to talk?"

"Not tonight, Angelena."

"But Papa—

"I'm tired. I'll see you in the morning. Gage," he called over his shoulder, "normal time tomorrow, please."

"Yes, sir."

Her father slowly climbed the stairs. He appeared ten years older tonight than he had this morning. She waited until she heard the door to his bedroom close.

"Are you regretting our little date today?"

She spun. Where Santo's voice had sent icy tendrils of fear through her, Gage's deep vocals sent spirals of need dancing along her body.

He prowled toward her, stalking her, the heat in his expression wiping away the memory of Santo's phone call.

"No." The anxiety she'd lived with for the past hour, slowly dissipated as a new emotion took hold.

Gage continued to close the distance between them.

She eventually found herself backed into the wall next to the entrance to the family room she'd just exited.

Gage stopped mere inches from her. He stood so close, warm puffs of his breath caressed her forehead and fluttered her bangs. He smelled faintly of coffee. "You know, Lena, until today, I thought you were wound as tight as that bun you so often wear. The opportunity to see you let loose of your strict control was a sight to behold. I can't wait for it to happen again." His gaze dipped to her mouth.

She licked her lips.

His eyes widened. His pupils darkened. His nostrils flared.

"Um…" Was this the opening she needed? Could she find a way to get Gage Barrett to marry her? Indecision battled within her. Their relationship would have to be discreet. She couldn't risk her father discovering her plan, such that it was. Their love had to be believable. She'd have to tell Gage the truth, though, eventually. If she laid it on the line, would he help her? Maybe she could pay him? She immediately discarded that idea. Talk about an indecent proposal. She needed to be married, but she didn't want to feel like a whore to make it happen.

Somehow, she'd make that trip down the aisle with Gage on her arm. Then she'd convince him to stick it out long enough to get the Giovanni and Santo off her back. Unfortunately, time wasn't on her side. She needed to get this engagement rolling. "Gage?"

He placed one large hand flat on the wall next to her head. "Yes?"

Her heart raced.

He leaned in closer. His eyes dropped to half-mast.

"I was wondering if…maybe…you might…"

He dipped his head to the right and brought his nose to the curve of her neck. He sniffed and nuzzled her skin. "You smell nice."

The whisper of his words tickled her skin. Goosebumps broke out along her body. She gulped.

"What were you wondering, Lena?"

God, his voice—low, raspy, sexy—made her think of tangled sheets and sweaty bodies. His tongue lightly traced the sweep of her ear. She moaned and tipped her head slightly. He sucked her lobe between his teeth and nipped. She gasped. "I was thinking that…" She swallowed. He tucked his face into the space between her shoulder and her head. His breath warmed her flesh. Her nipples hardened to achy points beneath her shirt. She wanted his hands on her. She couldn't stop from grasping his waist and clinging to his leather belt.

"Lena?"

"Hmm?" Wasn't she the one trying to ask him a question?

"Look at me."

She lifted her chin and opened her eyes, hesitant to see the look on his face, the desire she wished for in his eyes. When their gazes finally connected and locked, she couldn't hold back a groan at the ravenous look he gave her.

"I'm going to kiss you."

"Okay." Was there any other answer?

His slow and sexy smile stripped away her breath. His hooded eyes mirrored the passion coursing through her veins. All sorts of naughty thoughts crowded inside her head.

He brushed his lips lightly across hers. He didn't try to gain entry to deepen the kiss. He simply applied more pressure. He licked along her bottom lip and then the top. Then he pressed his mouth tight to hers.

Just as she was about to open to him, desperate for a taste, he was gone, taking his delicious heat with him. She opened her eyes. She didn't remember closing them. She blinked to regain clarity.

"I'd like to see you tomorrow."

"Okay." Wow, what a witty conversationalist. Her teachers would be so proud.

He smiled again, but this time it was quick and more amused than carnal. He backed up, swiveled on his heel, and walked toward the front door, the bottom of his fitted jacket caressing his tight ass.

She fisted her hands. "Hey, wait." The fog finally lifted, clearing her senses, presenting her with a larger vocabulary.

He turned and cocked an eyebrow.

"I thought you wanted a glass of water."

"I got what I came for." He gave her a cheeky wink. "Don't forget to lock the door and set the alarm." Then he was gone, the door closing with a soft click behind him.

Lena remained leaning against the wall. What had just happened? She gave her head a shake, pushed away and crossed the hallway to do as he'd told her.

Halfway up the stairs, on the way to her room, she paused and looked back to the front entrance. Perhaps getting him to fall for her would be much easier than she'd thought.

She just needed to remember she was in this for a short-term husband only. Not a friend. Certainly not a soul mate. She simply needed a marriage certificate with his signature on it.

Chapter Seven

"**G**ET IN." GAGE HELD THE LIMO'S DOOR WIDE OPEN. He'd overheard her and her father earlier and knew she planned to go for a run before starting some paperwork she had piling up. His first plan had been to sneak back into the house after dropping Vincent at work, search his office, and plant a listening device. But, after a traffic accident jammed the highway, he'd pulled up the driveway just in time to see her return. A week ago, he'd told her he wanted to see her. His job had kept him too busy to follow through. Now he finally had the chance, and couldn't resist the opportunity to spend a little time with her, get to know her better.

She stood a few feet away with one hand on the railing, one foot on the bottom step, contemplating him. She hadn't said no.

"I thought we could talk," he said.

"I could use a shower."

He could lick the sweat from her body. "I think you look fine."

The sheen on her skin and the rosy coloring to her cheeks enhanced her beauty. Her top clung to her breasts, outlining the dark sports bra she wore underneath it. Her shorts highlighted a killer set of legs. She shrugged, then joined him at the car.

He waited while she climbed in the back, his hands itching to mold her behind as she gave him a clear view of its beautiful shape. What color panties did she wear? Did she prefer cotton or silk? Sexy or functional? When all decked out for the day, did her bra match her panties?

He'd been such a jerk last week, teasing her like he did. He'd honestly needed a glass of water, but as soon as he'd seen her, the desire to kiss her became the only thought in his head.

Gage followed her inside the vehicle and shut the door, enclosing them in the spacious interior. The tinted windows dampened the heat of the morning sun. She swung around and dropped onto the seat nearest the driver's partition. In the confines of the car, her scent surrounded him. Hot female flesh. Sweat mixed with the deodorant she'd used. It made his blood sing.

She swiveled her head to the right and glanced toward the front entrance of the house.

"Your father's not in there."

"He's not?"

"Nope. I just got back from dropping him off downtown." Which she knew. She gave him a curious glance. She even batted her eyelashes. Wait a minute. Did the tables just turn? "Mary's gone too," he added, because he needed to fill the sudden awkward silence.

Her nose wrinkled in the cutest way and those gorgeous dark eyes sparkled with mischief. "Then why are we in the car?"

Because if they were in the house, he might be tempted to conduct a full search, first of the house and then of her. Or maybe the other way around. The look in her eyes and his body's reaction to it, spelled disaster. The kind where they'd both be naked in the back of the limo very soon. Gage shifted on the limo's bench seat.

Suddenly all his personal reasons for not having sex with her flew out the window. He'd just have to find a way to keep it objective. If he discovered something that conflicted with the case, he was man enough to step away from whatever it was that appeared to be happening here. Wasn't he?

"I do want to get to know you better," she said.

"You already asked me lots of questions the other day. I think it's my turn this time."

She crossed her arms over her chest, hiding nipples that poked at her shirt teasing him. "Okay then, Mr. Barrett. Ask me whatever you'd like."

"It's just Gage to you, Princess."

She pursed her lips.

Aha, the first question of this so-called meeting appeared from nowhere because he knew it annoyed the hell out of her. "Why don't you like me calling you Princess?"

She rolled her eyes. "Really? It's a label that doesn't fit me in the least."

"From where I sit, it's tailored for you."

"How can you say that?" She looked insulted. She unfolded her arms, placed a palm flat on either side of her thighs and leaned forward. "You've worked for my father for, what? Two months? In that *short* time, the other day was the first time we've spoken, beyond me providing you with destinations for my outings."

Perhaps they'd only begun conversing with words, but he'd noticed the discreet glances, and the covert once-overs she'd been giving him when she thought he wasn't watching. But Gage was always watching. Especially when such a stunning woman was nearby. One who might be involved in criminal affairs.

She settled back, but at least she didn't cover her chest again. She picked at the hem on her navy running shorts instead. "Other than knowing how much I love hamburgers, you don't know a thing about me."

He tipped his head. "Fair enough. So fill me in. Who is Angelena Bianco?"

She glanced out the window. "I'm twenty-nine and I went to Harvard."

"I knew that."

She snapped her head back to look at him. "How?"

He shrugged. "Your father told me."

Not quite true. Vincent had mentioned it when Gage first started working for him. The dossier he'd received months ago, long before becoming her father's drive, had covered the essentials. Since then he'd added to his personal version of the file with little tidbits he'd picked up along the way. Important things such as her favorite color was red, she looked stunning in pearls—though he'd love to see her in nothing but. She treated herself to mint-chocolate chip ice-cream when she was feeling blue, which happened more frequently than he liked. And she played with the dainty silver locket around her neck when she was nervous or scared.

Like she was doing now. The fact that she'd twined it around her finger and released it too many times to count, along with the quick pulse fluttering visibly in her throat, underscored the degree of nervous energy accumulating in her body.

"Well, besides that, I don't have much of a social life. I spend my time either working or at home."

"Why?"

She gave him a confused look. "Why what?"

"Why don't you have much of a social life?"

She turned away. A flush climbed up her neck and settled on her cheeks, noticeable even under her darker skin tone. She lifted one shoulder. "I don't know. Don't have anybody to go out with, I guess."

"No girlfriends? No boyfriends?"

"Nope."

"You're an attractive woman, Lena. I find that hard to believe."

"It is what it is."

Her file didn't list any long-lasting relationships in the past couple of years. "Don't women like to go shopping, eat at nice places and gossip?"

She narrowed her eyes at him. "I'm not a gossiper and I abhor shopping. I'll concede I do like nice restaurants though."

Wow. This girl wasn't typical, based on his experience with women. "Do you like music?"

She got a dreamy look in her eyes. "I love music."

"Who's your favorite?"

She signed and turned away again. "You'll laugh."

"Hardly."

"It's not your style."

"Who's the one making assumptions now?" he asked.

"Touché." She rolled her eyes, but he could tell by the way she fidgeted that it was a big deal to her. "I actually love all kinds of music, though I'm partial to classic rock." She hesitated, succulent lips parted. "But my first love is classical."

Interesting, but not surprising given her upbringing. "Who's your favorite composer?"

"Beethoven."

"Favorite piece?"

"Moonlight Sonata, of course. I can listen to that one over and over for hours on end."

He would play it for her repeatedly for hours on end.

She stroked the door handle. His cock twitched at the imagined sensation of her fingertips gliding along his skin in a similar feather-light caress. He coughed.

"What are we doing in here, Gage?" she asked him again.

He shifted on the seat, making room. What he wanted to do went against every grain of personal protocol. He could blame it on the case. Wade told him to get close to Lena to find out what she knew about her father's business dealings. He was only doing what his partner suggested. Wasn't he? Not likely.

His grandfather once told him to seize the day. Gage had been resisting that advice since the day he began this assignment and saw a picture of her. This attraction he felt had only gotten worse since that first time she'd thumbed her nose at him. So, today he would listen to his grandfather. Today he planned to seize the beautiful woman sitting across from him, the situation be damned. Because at the moment, he couldn't care less about her father.

Across the empty space between them, her chest rose and fell with each breath, her nostrils flaring slightly.

He raised his right hand and crooked his finger. "Come here, Lena."

* * *

The inside of the car suddenly felt ten degrees warmer. Lena swallowed.

"Please." He patted the leather seat next to him. "I don't bite."

Although she'd watched a myriad of expressions fly across his handsome face while he appeared to go through some inner conflict, the grin on his lips implied he'd decided on the best course of action. He patted the leather again.

Should she? This was exactly what she needed to happen, right? To build a relationship with him. To get him to marry her. She had no plans to fall in love. However, she couldn't simply jump into the fray either. That would look too suspicious, not to mention, a bit desperate. Which she was, but no need to advertise it. She had to at least show an appearance of disinterest. For a few weeks, or days. Hours.

Hell, who was she kidding? She needed to drag him as quick as she could to the front of that church. Might as well get on with it. Not like it was a serious hardship after all.

Gingerly and as graceful as possible in the back of a limo while wearing running gear and stinking like the three miles she'd run, Lena crossed the short space and settled next to Gage. His sheer size and presence overwhelmed her. She quivered in excitement.

She tried to keep as much distance between them as she could. She didn't want to mess up his uniform. Unfortunately, the bench seat was smaller than the other one and he took up lots of space. No matter how she moved, some part of her left side rubbed against him. And wow, did he smell so much better than her. Whatever scent he wore, she could spend the next hour with her nose wedged into the center of his chest or the curve of his neck. Which only edged the heat surrounding her up higher by a notch, or ten.

Her phone, tucked into her back pocket, rang out a melody indicating she'd just received a text message.

"Ignore it," Gage murmured. He faced her and stretched

one muscular arm along the top of the seat. He twined his fingers through her damp hair.

The play of his fingers created a tingle under her flesh. He was actually making her job easier by making the first move. She would start there. She could do this. She only needed it to be short lived anyway. She didn't plan to keep him.

With time not on her side, she'd work with what she had. She needed a husband before her father forced her into a marriage she didn't want. Gage Barrett was the best choice available for the position. Moreover, judging by the expression on his face, the flaring of his nostrils, and the way he kept shifting to get comfortable, the attraction was mutual. But she didn't want to appear too easy. "I'm not sure this is appropriate."

"Is the lady of the house lowering herself to play with the driver?"

She winced. "I don't consider you the hired help, Gage."

"That's exactly what I am, Princess."

She scowled. "I've asked you not to call me that."

He narrowed his eyes, but not before she gasped at the intensity of the interest burning there. "Prove I'm not the just the hired help," he whispered into the silent interior of the car.

Lena hadn't realized just how well the car blocked all exterior noise from entering the sanctum of the lush leather and carpeting. A hundred yards away, down the curving driveway, cars zipped by on the street. Each week a landscaping crew mowed the lawn and weeded the gardens, but today wasn't that day. No staff, no expected deliveries, nobody to question her motives. Other than herself.

He sat there, staring at her. His eyes dark, hungry orbs.

He sucked in a breath. So did she, to capture that clean scent of his again. It was like an aphrodisiac. She watched him watching her, as each waited for the other to initiate contact. Her gaze dropped to his lips. His kissable lips. There was a hardness to his jaw, his whole face, but his lips looked soft. Wanting. Tasty.

Lena canted forward, closing the distance between them. He was the one to beckon her over, but he hadn't attempted to bridge the gap.

She licked her lips and had the satisfaction of seeing his gaze dart to her mouth. She ran her tongue over them again, just to tease. To tempt. His breath fluttered over her eyes, down the curve of her nose, she was that close to him now. She lifted her lashes, and caught him staring at her. She saw her reflection in his pupils.

Shutting her eyes, she summoned her courage and removed the last remaining space between them. She pressed her lips to his.

At first he didn't respond. She did all the work. She brushed her mouth over his, licked the seam of his lips.

Just as she was about to capture his bottom one between her teeth, he kicked into action and opened his mouth the slightest bit. Taking advantage, after a very slight hesitation, she slipped her tongue inside. Mmm. He tasted like French roast. And strawberry jam. Cute. Yummy. She smiled.

She crept her right hand up his chest, dipped her fingers inside his uniform jacket and rested her palm over his heart. It thumped a strong beat beneath her hand.

He groaned into her mouth.

Elated that this excited him as much as it did her, she curled her fingers into the starched fabric of his white dress shirt, and shimmied closer to him, suddenly desperate to erase all empty air between them.

The arm he'd been resting along the seat slipped down to her ass and wrapped around her. Then he shifted again and smoothed his hand up her spine, until he cupped the back of her head.

She cringed slightly knowing how damp her skin must feel.

"What's wrong, Lena?"

"I'm just all sweaty. I'm sorry."

"Not an issue for me." He ran his tongue up the side of her bare neck. He nibbled along her jawline until he reached her mouth. Then he held her in place and angled his lips over hers, hovering for a couple of seconds before he drove his tongue deep inside.

Good God, Gage kissed like there was no tomorrow. And for her, there was definitely doubt. Maybe not in the twenty-four-hour definition, but certainly her future was in question.

Lena unfused her lips from his. They were both breathing heavy.

She could easily get carried away with a man like Gage. She needed to remind herself that Gage was a means to an end. A delightful means, for sure, but she couldn't allow herself to fall for him. She didn't want to end up like her father. She didn't want to end up alone. Maybe with a child that had only one mostly-absent parent to rely on. In her experience, no matter how much you loved somebody, you ended up one-half of the whole in the end. And the one left behind became a shell of their former self.

"Where did you go?" Gage peered down at her, his brow furrowed in concern.

"I'm sorry." She shut down her reflections, throwing up a thick wall to keep them at bay so she could concentrate on the here and now and her immediate future. The past was history, but her future needed to be rewritten, and she was determined to ensure she got to choose the plot herself. Starting right now.

Lena reached up and wrapped one arm around Gage's neck, pulling his head down to her. "My mind drifted for a moment, but I promise it won't happen again."

"Maybe I can help," he said.

She nodded. "I'm certainly hoping so, Gage."

Gage dropped his mouth back to hers and this time she focused entirely on him. On where he placed his hands at her hips, his thumbs circling over the silk of her shorts. On where he was locked to her, his tongue sweeping alongside hers. His taste mixed with hers. She let herself fall against his hard chest as he deepened the kiss.

Lost in the moment, Lena hardly noticed when he shifted his weight and pressed her back into the seat and further into a reclining position. Then his lips were gone from hers, but that was okay because now they were leaving a moist trail down her neck.

One of his hands worked under the hem of her shirt. She gulped, and he raised his head, his eyes asking all sorts of questions. She blinked slowly, nodded her head just enough for him to notice and then thankfully his mouth was back on her skin, following the path cleared as his fingers deftly rolled the material up until he came to her covered breasts. With a forceful tug, he pulled the bottom of her sports bra away from her midriff and pushed it up and over her boobs.

With her breasts bared, her top and bra mangled under

her armpits, she was a little uncomfortable. But she wasn't prepared to quit now. She yanked them over her head and tossed them aside. Somebody, hell, maybe both of them, moaned and made a grunt of satisfaction. Lena grabbed each side of his head, burying her fingers in his hair, holding him to her chest.

He licked a trail up her cleavage and over each mound, dragging his tongue over the hard tip before capturing it between his teeth and biting gently. When he covered her right nipple, his breath hot, she arched into him.

He raised his head. "Fuck, you're sexy. I never would have figured, Princess."

The first half of his statement sent a ripple of pleasure rolling over her. The second half caused her to stiffen. "I don't like you calling me that, Gage."

"I know you don't." He chuckled, the sound evil and sinful at the same time.

"Then why do you continue to do it?" she asked.

He sucked her breast into his mouth. At the same time, he inched his fingers over and pinched the tip on the other one.

She gasped.

He released her. "Tell me stop, Lena. Tell me you don't want this to happen."

The husky quality of his voice was unlike anything she'd ever heard from a man. He sounded desperate. Maybe just as desperate for her to do as he asked as he was for her to ignore his plea.

With no encumbrances, and no instructions from her to end this interlude, he looked deep into her eyes. Whatever he saw there drew a rough groan from his throat. He dropped his head back to the task, and licked a wet swatch between her two heaving breasts, moving back and forth, giving attention to each straining tip. "If we don't stop right now—"

Her phone chirped an incoming message.

Gage's tongue continued doing wicked things.

The phone chirped a second time. Growling, she slipped her hand into the back of her shorts to retrieve it. Glancing at it, she swiped the screen and touched her message app. Her eyes started to drift closed but sprang open again. Her attention zeroed in on the two messages she'd received. She opened the first one.

Hey babe. It's your future husband here.

Holy shit. She opened the second one.

Can't wait to finally have you.

This just got very real. A small part of her must have hoped it wasn't. She tensed.

Gage reared back. "Everything okay?"

No. Not at all. She swallowed, backed out of the message, and tossed the phone to the other side of the limo.

"Please don't stop, Gage. That's not what I want."

But he had stopped. His dark eyes pinned her in place. "You're sure?"

She nodded. She was damn sure. Now more than ever.

Chapter Eight

THE SWEET TASTE OF HER FLESH SEARED ITSELF ONTO HIS taste buds. Her scent invaded his pores. Gage was so fucking hard, one innocent touch and he'd go off like a rocket.

Despite his intent to take his grandfather's advice, he really hadn't intended for things to go this far when he'd invited her to join him inside the limo. She'd drawn him in with her innocent look and alluring smell. The scent of her body after a workout was such a fucking turn on, just being near her made him feel alive.

Normally he showed more restraint during a case, had no problem keeping his distance, no matter how beautiful the temptation. Clearly, he'd gone too long without sex. After a self-imposed hiatus, that side of his brain was too excited to go back into a resting state. Once he'd kissed her, inhaled her arousal after she'd exerted herself, all bets were off.

Gage wrapped his lips around one sweet, brown, pebbled nipple and sucked. Her groan sent a surge of satisfaction racing through him. He slipped his free hand down her torso and ran his fingers across her thigh to the short inside seam of her shorts. Dipping his fingers beneath the soft material, he encountered an even softer thigh. He slid his hand along her inner leg, the warmth her pussy radiated, encouraging him to inch closer.

When he reached the apex of her thighs, he encountered her panties. He passed the tips of two fingers over the gusset. Nicely damp.

She lifted her hips.

Gage fit a finger beneath the edge of the cotton. Just as he closed his eyes and slowly dragged his tongue over one of her nipples, he ran his finger along her slit, dipping between her pussy lips into her moisture. He groaned and plunged his finger deep, pumping it in and out a few times before adding a second one. The fantasy of what she'd feel like around his cock made him growl.

"God, Lena, I want to taste you. Are you okay with that?"

She didn't respond and he looked up, his breath catching in his throat at the gorgeous sight. He stared at her in awe. Her head was thrown back, her neck stretched taut; her eyes closed leaving her dark lashes to fan out across her cheekbones. She was biting her bottom lip, all the color gone. Awesome.

He smiled, satisfaction zinging through him. Shit, if that little bit of play affected her in such a way, how would she react when he truly got down to business?

Playing to his curiosity, Gage pressed a kiss to each breast before working his way down her belly, leaving a trail of them all the way to her center. He dropped to his knees on the floor between her thighs, grabbed the waist of her shorts, and jerked them and her underwear over her hips and down her legs, until they cleared her runners.

He lifted her right leg, and laid his lips to the inside of her delicate ankle.

She squeaked.

He hushed her and then made his way up her leg, leaving faint love bites in hidden areas. One behind her knee, one on her inner thigh, midway to her pussy. Far enough away to tease her, too close to tempt him, he stopped and rested that leg over his shoulder. Then he started again with her other leg, beginning with a tender kiss to that ankle.

By the time he reached her upper thigh, she was panting. His breathing sounded harsh. His heart beat a loud rhythm inside his chest. The scent of her arousal tantalized him, making his mouth water.

Gage glanced up her body. She'd dipped her chin and was watching him. Her eyes were large, dark pools of desire. Her cheeks flushed pink beneath her olive skin. At some point she'd released her hair, and now it hung in a sexy, messy mop around her head. Just as he'd imagined.

Anticipation fueled her expression. He had no desire to disappoint her.

Keeping his eyes trained on her, Gage started at the bottom and ran his tongue up through her slit, gathering her wetness and licking his way to her clit. He flicked the top of it.

She jumped.

"Jesus, Lena. You taste delicious." Tangy and so fucking good, her flavor settled over his tongue. She became his new favorite dish.

Gage continued to tickle her clit with his tongue, taking great pleasure in each buck of her hips, each whispered plea that fell from her lips. He nibbled at her plump flesh. He laid kisses along her lips. He pushed a finger into her pussy and pumped it slowly in and out, each time enjoying the clutch and release of her body. She sucked him in, refused to let him loose. Like he wanted to go anywhere.

"Gage, I can't—"

"I want to make you come, Lena."

She moaned.

Gage lapped at her in earnest, plunging two fingers deep

inside her at the same time, curling them to stroke her sweet spot. When she began thrashing, he laid one arm across her hips, holding her down while he pumped his fingers in and out and sucked her clit between his lips.

"Oh, God, Gage, I'm going to come."

He raised his gaze, intent on watching her fall apart, anxious to see the pleasure cross her face at the exact moment she let go.

Lena's face contorted with what looked like a mix of intense satisfaction and agony.

The only thing better than seeing that look on her face would be watching it firsthand while he was buried as deep as possible inside her.

Gage softened his touch as she relaxed. When she slumped against the seat, he rose, braced an arm on either side of her and leaned over her slumped body.

Her eyes fluttered, her lids rising slowly. Her skin glowed. A cute grin settled on her lips.

He smiled and rubbed his hands up and down her legs.

She opened her eyes and peered up at him. "Wow."

He chuckled. "Should I say you're welcome?"

She laughed. "That felt nice. Very nice."

"I'm glad." He backed away as she struggled to sit up.

Her expression changed to one of uncertainty. "Um, don't you want to…?"

He waved her unfinished comment away. "No. I'm good."

She looked crestfallen, so he rushed to put her at ease. Gage took her hands in his. "Believe me, Lena. I want nothing more to take this further, but I don't want to do that in the back of a car. I'd much rather have you spread out in a nice big bed, when we have lots of time, and no chance of interruptions."

She dropped her gaze to their laps.

"I'm not saying no, honey. I'm saying I can hold out for a while longer."

Her phone chirped yet again and she went rigid. She glowered at the device.

His own phone chose that moment to vibrate in his pocket. He released one of her hands and pulled it out of his pocket. He checked the display. Shit. It was Wade. He couldn't talk to his partner in front of Angelena, but he also couldn't ignore the call in case it was something important.

Gage hit the call button and spoke. "Hey there. I can't talk right now. Can I call you back in a few minutes?"

"Sure. Everything okay?" Wade asked

"Yeah." Gage glanced at Angelena.

She stared straight back at him while she tucked herself back into her bra and shirt.

This woman was making an impression on him, and he wasn't sure how he felt about that.

Wade coughed on the other end, pulling his attention back to the case. "Any news on your end?" he asked.

"Maybe."

That caught Gage's attention. Did they finally have a lead? He checked his watch. "I can be at your place in thirty minutes."

Lena pouted.

"Sounds good," Wade said. "I'll throw a couple of burgers on the grill and I can debrief you on what we've got while we eat."

"I'll be there." Gage ended the call and put the phone back in his pocket. Then he looked at Lena. "I'm sorry. But I need to go."

"Was that my father?"

He rubbed this hand over his face. "No. It was the guy who runs the limousine service. I need to head over there and take care of a few things before your father needs me to head downtown to pick him up."

A look of uncertainty passed over her face. "Oh. Sure. No problem." She crawled across the car, grabbed her phone, opened the door, and climbed out before he could stop her.

He hurried after her. "Listen, Lena. I really am sorry. But this is work."

"No, Gage, honestly, I understand. I've got things to do anyway." She stood outside the car, looking rumpled in an I-just-had-a-great-orgasm-in-the-back-of-a-limo way, and slightly uncomfortable about what to do next. She probably wondered where they went from here.

He knew exactly where he wanted to go, and it wasn't to sit in Wade's backyard and eat a hamburger. "Can I take you anywhere?"

She shook her head. "No. I'm fine. I have some work to do."

Gage mentally calculated the time to drive to Wade's, get briefed, and then head downtown for Vincent.

"Don't worry about me, Gage. I'm a big girl. You better get going if you don't want to be late."

If they'd finally made some headway with Soranno, then he really did need to go. That took priority. Giovanni Soranno needed to be hauled off the street and put behind bars. And Gage Barrett was just the man to make that happen.

Chapter Nine

LENA PUSHED THE HEAVY EXTERIOR GLASS DOOR OPEN, and stepped aside to allow a young mother with a stroller to enter. Outside she breathed in a huge, humid lungful of New York air. The stench of garbage past it's pick up point lodged deep in her throat, almost gagging her. Fantastic. She'd taste that for the rest of the day, thank you very much.

She took another deep breath, hating that she had to, but after the meeting she'd just had with her father, she needed to calm her racing heart. Time was running out. Santo apparently believed he was wooing her.

After her stolen moment with Gage inside the limo, she'd gone into the house to shower. She'd tossed her phone to the bed as though it had burned her, refusing to ruin what had just happened. Unable to ignore it forever though, she'd relented once she was dressed and scanned the messages. Santo had somehow found her phone number and thought it would be cute to send her an image of what she'd be getting when they got married. The image was scorched into her brain.

To make matters worse, she'd also found an extravagantly wrapped package addressed to her sitting on the dining table when she went downstairs for breakfast. Thinking it might be from her father as a means of apologizing, she'd opened it to discover a silver tennis bracelet. The note declared it an engagement present from Santo.

She'd called a cab and headed straight to her father's office with the intention of begging him to call this asinine thing off. But the trip had been a total waste. When she'd complained about the bracelet from Santo, her father had looked incredulous and said he'd thought the gift was a nice gesture. Then he'd asked if she'd connected with the wedding planner yet. She'd wanted to scream. No. In fact, she'd deleted the ten email messages the woman had left. Her father hadn't been happy with that news and scolded her like he would a child. Damn it. She had no intention of going through with the wedding, so she saw no reason to talk to a wedding planner. She refused to do anything that would encourage either her father or Santo.

The oddest thing was that every word out of his mouth sounded forced. Not once did he look her in the eye as he espoused the virtues of the Soranno family.

She needed to marry Gage and then this whole mess with Santo and his father would go away. If only she could simply walk up to him and say, "Hey, Gage, do a girl a favor and marry her so she doesn't have to wed a crude, disgusting bully."

Lena looked around. Wall Street was jammed packed. People rushed everywhere in cities, but she always found that statement to be the truest here. Because money was made here? Stocks traded? Investments planned? Deals cut? Marriages arranged without the bride's permission?

People hustled in both directions, most so absorbed in their own little world, they'd tuned out everything else. A car horn blasted, somebody yelled and a bus rolled to a stop at the corner to spit people out and swallow a few more.

The last thing Lena wanted to do right now was show a

house, but while she'd been with her father, she'd received two calls that she'd sent straight to voice mail at the time, fearful it would be Santo. When she'd found the courage to check, the first was for a last-minute showing. It happened to be an unoccupied model home, so at least she wasn't inconveniencing any owners. Unfortunately, she didn't have time to head home first, so she stepped up to the curb to hail a cab.

"Well hello there, my beautiful bride."

Lena shrieked and spun around. Her worst nightmare stood in all his disgusting glory right behind her. "Santo. I thought you were out of the country."

"And here I thought my fiancé would be happy to see me. Did you like my pretty present? I picked it out just for you." He leered at her.

"I'm not marrying you." In many instances, clothes made the man, but not in Santo Soranno's case. He may have dressed as if he had money, but he sure as hell didn't speak or behave as if he did.

"I'm inclined to say otherwise, sweet cheeks. I, for one, cannot wait for our special day."

"Look, Santo. My father said we'd be married on Labor Day. So I assumed I'd have until then."

"Oh, I'll give you until then, baby. I just want to make sure you don't forget me in the meantime."

A dingy yellow city owned taxi screeched to a halt next to her, the driver shaking his fist at another cabbie who'd tried to snag the fair.

Santo laughed. The sound rang insane to her ears.

She need to get away from him right now. She yanked the back door open and jumped into the cab, slamming the door shut, putting a barrier between her and Santo. Not taking her eyes off him, she gave the driver the address. "Hurry, please."

The cabbie pulled away, leaving the devil himself standing on the curb, still laughing.

Lena released a shaky breath and settled back for the long drive. Maybe by the time she reached her destination, the shaking would stop. In the meantime, she remembered the other voice mail and replayed it in her head, a voice she hadn't heard for years, one of the few friends she'd had at high school.

People often considered her attitude toward money to be aloof and conceited, but they couldn't be further from the truth. Money just never mattered to her. What child didn't want to grow up in a home surrounded by a wooden fence with a dog in the back yard and a cat on the porch? Maybe a swing set. Friends to play with. Two parents. Her mother in the kitchen baking cookies while Lena and her best friend monitored a lemonade stand on the sidewalk. Her idyllic childhood. The stuff dreams were made of.

Instead of playing in the sandbox, or on swings at the park with other kids in the neighborhood, she'd been raised in a private school. Away during the week, home on weekends. Her father at work, while she played quietly in her room, under the care of the housekeeper. She loved Mary, but she'd needed a mother, playmates, and a true childhood.

Her father was far from wealthy. He simply made a good salary and spent it on nothing frivolous. They had a nice home and that was it. He'd insisted she go to a private school. His way of giving her friends.

Sadly for her, all the kids at her school had their own lives, their own cliques. They had looked at her funny and kept their distance, knowing she wasn't really a rich kid. Simply a well-dressed one.

The only girl to ever befriend her had been Rosa Soranno. Rosa didn't have friends then either, but the two of them had two things in common. Their fathers worked together, and neither of them had a mother. Rosa's had died when she was ten, so at least she had solid memories, something Lena had envied.

Even though a couple of years separated them in age, they'd hung out at lunch or in the library together. But they never saw each other outside of school. After all these years, Rosa was calling, asking Lena to please return her call. There'd been a sense of urgency in her tone.

To this day, Lena had no true friends. The few women she occasionally met for lunch were from the real estate office she seldom frequented, considering most of her work could be done from home.

She may not understand her father's world, or have any interest in it. But Lena felt compelled to admit she was curious. Rosa's timing intrigued her. Lena knew Rosa wasn't a fan of her own father or brother. She'd never told Lena why, but Rosa often shared her plans to leave home as soon as she possibly could. As soon as she could get out from under her father's thumb.

Did Rosa know something?

Lena pulled her phone from her purse and returned Rosa's call. It went straight to voice mail. "Hi Rosa. It's Angelena Bianco. I got your voice mail. I must say, I'm curious as to your timing. I'd really like to talk with you, so try me again, or I'll call again later today. Bye."

Crap. Cars, people and buildings pass by outside the car's

window. She already missed being with Gage, but she actually enjoyed the opportunity to be alone for a little while. Her father never drove, always preferred to use the car service, insisting it allowed him to work to and from work. He had no other hobbies. He didn't even read or watch television. She felt sad for him, because he'd never moved on after her mother died.

As the driver left the downtown core and hit the highway toward her destination, she contemplated what she perceived to be her only viable option out of this mess. The ringing of her phone cut her off cut off her thoughts too soon. Thinking it might be Rosa, she answered without glancing at the display.

"Hello?" She glanced toward the front, catching the driver looking back at her through the mirror.

"Running off from your soon-to-be-husband like that wasn't very nice. Especially when I rushed home just to see you."

She went still. "Santo," she said on an exhale that he probably mistook for breathless need.

"You never told me if you liked your present."

She swallowed. Her palms grew damp.

"I can't wait to see it on you, baby."

"What do you want?"

He chuckled, the sound grating on her nerves, sending shivers down her spine. "Fuck, babe. You can't be that naïve. I bet you liked that picture I sent, too. Just wait until it's your hand wrapped around my cock. Fuck. I'm picturing it now and it's making me horny as hell. Bet you give good head."

Her stomach somersaulted. She must have made a sound because the driver's eyes squinted in concern and he tossed her a look over his shoulder. She ducked her chin and turned toward the window. "Look, Santo, it's not a good time right now."

"Well, babe, I won't keep you then. I just wanted to give you a taste of what you can expect being with me. You won't have to work no more either. You'll be able to wait at home for me. And oh, what fun we will have."

Had he just smacked his lips? She shuddered, quickly hit end, and closed her eyes.

She needed to step things up with Gage. She had zero time. No way in hell could she wait for two months. She needed to find a way to end this sooner, because she didn't think she could last until Labor Day.

Chapter Ten

"APPARENTLY VINCENT'S FIRM IS PLANNING ANOTHER client appreciation event and Soranno is invited." Wade flipped the burgers and then sat back down at the picnic table across from him. He took a sip of his beer.

"How can you be sure?" Gage asked. It's not like this was the first time Soranno had been invited to one of Vincent's affairs. It wouldn't even be the first time he'd actually shown up. The problem was he managed to get in and out without notice most of the time. They'd never caught him in the middle of any transactions even remotely suspicious. He glad-handed with the best of them, coming across as the consummate executive. Any nefarious dealings happened out of range of whatever eyes and ears they managed to get in place. Which to date had frustrated the fuck out of Gage.

Wade grinned like the cat that caught the canary. "Because this time, we've managed to intercept the invitation, so we'll know when he's expected to arrive."

Now Wade had his attention.

"And we know what his business plans are while he's there."

Gage's jaw dropped open. "Seriously? They actually spelled it out in an email?" Talk about a major screw up on their part.

A pinched look crossed Wade's face. "Not the specifics. But enough that we know something is definitely in the works."

"Why don't you tell me exactly what we do know?"

Wade took another pull of his beer. "We managed to get

a quick peek at the email that went to Soranno inviting him to the party."

"And how did you do that?"

"I've been getting to know a few of the staff and I sweet talked Vincent's secretary into stepping away from her computer long enough that I was able to take a spin through her outgoing email. Vincent has arranged a private meeting at Soranno's request for nine thirty. They're supposed to be discussing two things. One has something to do with a new business he just acquired and the other is something he referred to as Labor Day."

"An actual business or a front for his laundering? Or a fictitious one? And what the hell does Labor Day mean?" Gage asked. Was it code for something other than a long weekend in September?

"No specifics on either were given," Wade replied.

"Damn it, Wade. I can't sit by and let this bastard get away with the things he does. He sells drugs to kids. He kills people." Most of the time, not by his own hand, but it didn't matter. He gave the orders. Gage knocked back a drink of his beer and then slammed his bottle down on the table.

"We'll catch him, Gage. Sooner or later he'll make a mistake."

"Yeah, like the one that killed my brother?" Gage hopped up and paced the deck. He scrubbed his hand through his hair. "I don't want to watch another set of parents go through what mine did, Wade. I refuse to give up until that man is behind bars where he belongs, where he can't hurt anybody again."

Every day Giovanni freely walked the streets, he hurt families. His dealers sold drugs to children on street corners. His thugs threatened store owners to pony up protection money. The more money Giovanni Soranno made on the streets, the more cash Vincent siphoned through a network of small legitimate businesses that Giovanni owned, free and clear.

"About that…"

Gage snapped his head up. "About what?"

Wade fidgeted with the label on his beer bottle. He dropped his gaze and looked at his plate. Then he took a deep breath and raised his head to stare Gage in the eyes. He didn't blink.

Gage couldn't look away. His gut churned. "Just say it."

Wade finally broke the connection. "The team back at the office have been backtracking through Soranno's businesses. Tracking the money."

"Yeah, I know that. Did they find something?"

Wade nodded. "That store where your brother was killed was one of Soranno's."

"We already knew that."

"Yeah, but we didn't know he was using it as his over-the-counter pharmacy. It was his home base, Gage. Nor did we know he'd purposely set up one of his runners who was swindling him to be taken out that day."

Gage stopped breathing for five solid seconds. His heart raced.

"In their digging, they found a statement from a witness. A statement that was buried. It was never publicized."

"What did it say?"

"Apparently it contained a detailed description of the shooter."

Gage frowned. "The gangbanger."

Wade shook his head slowly. "No. The gangbanger took

the blame. But the shooter was Giovanni himself. He was sending a message."

And Gage's younger brother, out running an errand for their mother, had been caught in the crossfire of the memo.

Gage stood with is feet shoulder width apart and his hands crossed behind his head, his fingers locked tight together. He sucked in great gulps of air, willing the anger to stay centered but in control. He didn't want to lose it now. He'd save that treat for Giovanni.

"We need to get into that room before nine so we can set up a couple of cameras and recorders," Wade said from behind him. "Once we have their meeting on tape, then we'll be able to ask for the warrant we need to search Vincent's office, finally get permission to tap his phones at home and at work. If Vincent uses a cell phone, we can tap that too."

Maybe they'd find the links to Soranno they were after, and could begin making their move to take the bastard down.

"Do we know where the party's going to be held?" Gage asked as he returned to his chair. He needed to put his brother's death aside for the moment and focus on the end goal. It was years ago, when Giovanni was younger. Gage hadn't even known who was behind it at the time. But Giovanni's day would come. Gage had lost almost everything that night. His brother and his family, but never his sense of purpose.

Wade got up and strolled to the grill, checked the meat and lifted them off, along with the corn he'd cooked. He put everything on a platter, turned off the barbecue and returned to the table. "At the downtown office, in their large boardroom."

"Well, that should make it a little easier to get in," Gage murmured.

"Not based on the additional security Soranno asked for. I'm hoping we can work around that, maybe get a couple of our own men to act as extra hands. I'm going to try to find a place to hide near his office. I can't imagine they'd conduct business in a crowded open area."

They quietly prepared their burgers, added a cob of corn to their plates and dished up some store-bought potato salad from the container Wade had placed on the table earlier. A fresh beer, a few bites of food in their stomachs and they resumed their conversation.

Gage set his knife and fork down. "When's the party?"

"End of the month. I've already talked to the boss and got an extension. He's willing to give us until after the party to wrap this up."

"So we have three weeks, four at best?"

"We can make it happen, Gage. I'll chat up the secretary some more and see what details I can get. I'll survey the floor plan and find a few guys who can get in there. You work the daughter. I still think there's something there."

Gage gripped his beer bottle in a crushing fist. He had no intention of working the daughter. Although he knew he should consider her suspicious and potentially a player in Giovanni's game, he just couldn't let himself believe that she was involved in anything corrupt. "You let me worry about Angelena." He checked the time. "Speaking of which, I need to head out. Vincent is expecting me to pick him up in about an hour and a half and it will take me most of that time to work my way through traffic."

"Does he have any more late night meetings planned?" Wade asked.

"Not that I'm aware of." Gage stood and grabbed his plate.

Wade followed suit. He strode across Wade's small deck and in through the patio door that needed a serious grease job. He dumped the waste and set his plate in the sink. "Thanks for dinner."

"No problem. Your turn next time," Wade added.

Gage left his friend, climbed into the limo, and settled in for the drive into town. At least he was heading against the major traffic flow. If luck happened to be on his side, Vincent would be in a talkative mood tonight.

He made it into the downtown core without too much trouble. As usual, he called when he was fifteen minutes away from the office tower, and Vincent was waiting for him in front of the building, ready to climb into the car as soon as Gage pulled to the curb. "Did you have a good day, Mr. Bianco?"

"Yes."

"The traffic coming into town wasn't too bad so I expect the drive back to be relatively quick. I should have you home in forty minutes, tops."

"That's good."

He apparently wasn't in a talkative mood.

"I understand your office is hosting a party at the end of the month." It was a huge gamble, but Gage was losing patience with this assignment. He needed to shove things along.

Vincent glanced up, his eyes shuttered. "How do you know that?"

Gage shrugged in a non-committal way. "I think I heard you mention it at some point. Or, maybe your daughter said something about it when I spoke with her this morning. Can't remember exactly." Fuck, he hoped she knew about it.

Vincent gave him a strange look, like he was flipping through his memory of events and conversations. He must have finally decided either scenario was plausible. "Yes, I am."

"Do you need me to pick up any of the guests for you, sir? I'd be happy to do that."

Shifting his attention between the traffic in front of him and the rear view mirror, Gage watched Vincent flounder through the conversation.

Generally, Gage didn't engage in idle chitchat. Neither did Mr. Bianco.

"I haven't thought that far ahead yet," the older man said. "But the company you work for would allow you to do that?"

"Sure why not? I'm under contract to you twenty-four-seven. I can pick up whoever you want me to." Gage hoped he'd go for it. Soranno had his own car and driver, but maybe he and Wade could find a way to disable that option. "I'm just putting it out there, sir, in case any of your guests are interested. I'm sure some of your more important guests may enjoy the convenience."

Vincent waved his hand in the air. "I'll think about it and let you know."

The rest of the trip passed in silence. Vincent eventually raised the partition and Gage tuned the radio to a local news station. He'd be glad when this case was over and he could move on.

A mental image of Angelena splayed out on the seat behind him, her legs over his shoulders, his face tucked nicely between her thighs distracted him for a moment. He'd like more of that first. He'd like to discover all her pleasure spots, taste and test each and every one of them. Find the ones that turned her to mush, the ones that made her wild.

He wanted to watch her come apart all over him, drown him in her desire. Hear her scream his name, beg him to let her come. He wanted to watch over her while she slept and regained her strength for round two.

But until this case was over, and he'd put another criminal who destroyed lives behind bars, he needed to focus on the case. Damn, it was hard, considering he saw her daily.

At least when he'd only had pictures and surveillance video to keep him occupied, he'd been able to remind himself of his objective, which wasn't to get laid by a stunningly beautiful woman. Unfortunately, the moment her scent waved under his nose, he'd had trouble keeping his goals in the forefront of his mind. Instead, he constantly thought about places and ways to fuck her.

Gage pulled off the highway and began making his way through the neighborhood streets toward the section of town where the Bianco's lived. He passed an elementary school with a parking lot packed full of cars and a bunch of kids decked out in soccer gear ambling between the vehicles and over by the schoolyard.

As they got closer to the area where Vincent and Angelena lived, the homes grew larger but the sense of community diminished.

Finally, he pulled into Vincent's driveway and drove around to the front of the house. He stopped, and then got out. Vincent was already out of the car by the time he got around to the side.

"Is there anywhere else you need to go this evening, sir?"

Vincent shook his head. "No. I'm staying in for the rest of evening." He started walking up the stairs to the front door, paused halfway, and turned back. "But Angelena sent me a message letting me know that she'd be showing a house. She took a cab. Perhaps you could go and get her?"

He really shouldn't. "Do you have the address?"

"Come in and I'll have Mary find it for you."

Gage followed him up the stairs and into the house. He waited in the entryway until Mary arrived with a piece of paper in her hand and a knowing and devious smile on her charmingly weathered face. "Hello, Gage."

"Mary." He liked Mary. Since he'd started working for the Biancos, she'd been feeding him. She'd also been making hints about him and Angelena. He'd found them amusing at the time. Now they took on a completely new meaning.

Her eyes twinkled when she looked up at him. "Lena is showing a house over in the new development. She should be finished by seven." She clasped her hands together in front of her and rocked back on her heels.

He fought a smile. "Is that right?"

"Yes. But I think you should try to get there by six thirty so you don't miss her."

"I can do that."

"Good. I'll be gone by the time you drop her off, and I'm sure her father will already have retired for the night, so take your time."

He chuckled. "Now why would I want to do that, Mary?"

She shrugged. "Oh, I don't know. She could use some free time, maybe some excitement. Take her for a drive. It's going to be a nice night." The cheeky woman winked at him, then turned and headed back to the kitchen, humming.

Gage tucked the piece of paper in his trouser pocket and returned to the car. He'd have to leave right away to catch Lena before she decided to call a cab.

Then he'd see if maybe this time he could keep his hands to himself.

Chapter Eleven

ANGELENA WANDERED AROUND THE FIRST FLOOR OF THE extravagant model home. Normally, her favorite part of showing a house was after the prospective buyers left. She'd walk through the empty home and imagine it filled with her things. Her fantasy furnishings changed with the style of the house, but every single piece was of her choosing, based on her preferences.

She also used the time to see the home through the eyes of her clients, experience what they saw, what they liked, what they didn't. She'd put her observations together with the comments they'd made and use that information when trying to close the sale, or look for other comparable options for them.

Tonight, she'd walked through the showing on autopilot. With every step throughout the house, her only thoughts were of Santo. His gift, his disgusting photo, the telephone conversation, the text messages, his surprise appearance. Everything confirmed her initial reaction to her father's announcement. Nothing anybody could ever say or do would convince her to go through with this marriage.

She continued her stroll through the unoccupied home. This particular house was luxury at its finest in a family oriented neighborhood. The builder had incorporated a number of upgrades, ratcheting up the cost of the house significantly. It had every modern convenience conceivable. It didn't suit her personal taste at all.

Most of the time Angelena envisioned herself in a small cottage-type home surrounded by a white picket fence. It would be open concept and filled with comfortable furniture you could sink into, curl up in on a rainy day and read a book. She'd have a back deck with patio furniture and a barbecue. A place she could sit on a warm summer's night and look up at the stars while she listened to the crickets.

Every aspect of her dream home was the complete opposite of what she'd grown up with. And she wanted it with every fiber of her being. But if her father and Santo had their way, she'd be confined to a mausoleum of a home, a virtual prisoner to a man comfortable talking to her like he owned her, offering lewd suggestions on a daily basis, and essentially making her feel like a whore.

Angelena crossed through the formal dining room, glancing up at the white floral crystal chandelier, and entered the enormous front foyer featuring an elegant staircase to the second level. A movement on the front porch captured her attention. Thinking it was her clients returning, she crossed the room to the front door. She paused when her cell phone rang. After her last phone call she wasn't sure she should answer, but it was the damn wedding planner again.

"Hello?"

"Ms. Bianco?"

"Yes."

"Hello, Ms. Bianco, may I call you Angelena?"

No, but the woman didn't pause long enough for Lena to tell her that.

"It's Sonia, your wedding planner, dear, and I have such fabulous ideas that I really need to discuss with you."

Lena wanted to hit her head against the wall. "Oh, gosh,

I'm really sorry, Sonia, but I'm at work right now and it's not a good time to talk." She rolled her eyes, ready to end the call. Somebody was becoming insistent on the doorbell.

"Well, dear, I can certainly understand that, however—"

"Gotta go, Sonia. We'll talk another time." Lena ended the call and yanked open the front door. "Gage? What are you doing here?" He looked gorgeous standing there, all uniformed up and expectant. Safe. A man she felt comfortable around, which seemed to be a rare occurrence these days.

"Hello, Angelena. Thought I'd give you a ride home."

One hand on the door handle, the other on the door casing, she blocked his entry. But bracing herself had nothing to do with denying him access and everything to do with restraining herself from falling to her knees before him and begging for a repeat of the performance he'd provided earlier.

She still felt his tongue gliding along her sex, his warm breath, his hard fingers plunging inside her as he grazed her clit with his teeth and brought her to orgasm.

He'd given her everything she'd needed and took nothing for himself, which only made her want to return the favor even more.

"Your father didn't want you taking a cab on your own late at night."

Immediately, her conversation with Santo drifted to the forefront of her mind. If she thought for one minute Santo was nearby, she'd probably be worried, but he probably stayed in the city.

She scoffed. "It's hardly late and I'm pretty sure I've mentioned that at my age, I'm quite cable of doing most things an adult can do."

Gage narrowed his eyes and studied her. "He only cares about you."

"I know," she conceded. "But he's treating me as a child and not letting me make my own decisions."

He frowned. "Such as?"

She needed a distraction and Gage was the perfect solution. She waved his comment away and turned into the house, beckoning him to follow. "Never mind. I'm almost finished."

The door shut behind her. Although she didn't turn around again, she felt him there, at her back, his warmth wrapping around her, making her feel secure and cozy. She liked cozy.

"I watched your clients drive away. What do you have left to do?"

She couldn't remember. She hardly recalled her conversation with the couple interested in the house. "I just need to walk through the house and make sure everything is as it should be before I lock up."

He looked impressed. "Would you like me to wait here?"

She let her gaze roam over his body. He certainly wore a uniform well. All she wanted to do was strip it off him.

"If you'd prefer. Or you can walk with me if you'd like." Frankly, having him nearby made her feel protected, and it gave her a chance to spend more time with him.

She climbed the stairs, a thrill of excitement shooting through her when she heard his footfalls trailing a few steps behind as she glided from room to room in the furnished but uninhabited home. His presence added to her distracted state, and she found herself picturing her and Gage living here, playing house in each room she entered.

When they walked into the master bedroom, they faced a beautiful bay window overlooking the back yard. Dense trees ringed the property and provided privacy from all angles. This was an estate lot, so the closest neighbor, once the development was finished and occupied, would be over one hundred feet away.

To the right of the double doorway was a walk-in closet the size of a small bedroom, and a master bath outfitted in stunning black granite and gold. The furnishings would appeal to most women, but she only had eyes for the massive canopy bed, the showpiece in the room. Sheer, airy drapes hung from the four corners of the dark wood posts. Plump gold pillows lay on top of the pristine white linens and covered the head of the bed.

Gage cleared his throat.

Lena swallowed around a lump in hers.

"Nice room."

"Gorgeous," she replied automatically. "Not my style though."

He snorted, the sound distinctly one of disbelief.

She paused and turned to him. "No, really. This isn't what I'd want at all."

"Seriously? I thought all rich kids liked to live the lifestyle," he said.

She shook her head. "I'm not rich, Gage. My father is simply frugal. He certainly hasn't lavished me with gifts. The stuff in that house are things my mother picked out. He's changed nothing since she died. Nothing there is mine, or for that matter, even his."

"So if this isn't your thing, what is?"

She shrugged. "Simple. I don't need all this." She swept her arm around the room. "I just need a clean, well-built home, a functional kitchen, a couple of bedrooms. I'd love to sit out on a deck at the back of my house and look out over a backyard landscaped with gardens I created myself."

He gave her a wide-eyed look of surprise and she laughed aloud.

"Told you I wasn't a princess. I don't even require stainless steel appliances and granite counter tops, though I'll admit, I wouldn't turn them down if they came with the place."

Gage cocked his head and scrutinized her. He gave her the oddest look, one she couldn't begin to decipher. He moved toward her, stalking her until the back of her knees slammed into the edge of the bed.

She thought of her plan, very aware that with Santo back in town already, she was quickly running out of time.

She plopped down with a bounce on the firm mattress. Her heart raced. She didn't fear Gage. She feared not being able to find a man like him. She had no desire to spend the rest of her life chained to a family and a man she loathed, receiving taunting emails, voicemails and gifts on a regular basis.

Gage chuckled, the sound deep and sexy, creating all sorts of warm tingles that raced along her flesh, doing a decent job of taking her mind off Santo.

He moved between her knees, nudging them apart.

She flattened her palms on the bed on either side of her.

"Since this isn't really your kind of place, how about we sully it up a little?" he suggested, his eyes alight with a mix of mischief and lust.

"I'm not sure that's a good idea." And yet, she looked around the staged room. There were no other showings planned for tonight. She had the only key. "Did you lock the door?"

Gage smiled wickedly. "I did."

Lena brushed her concerns and worry aside. She needed to take control of her future. Tonight she needed to make her own choice, do what she wanted to do. Right now she had a man who wanted her. And she desperately needed to feel wanted by somebody who she was just as attracted to.

She laid back just as Gage lowered himself over her, caging her between his muscled arms. She gulped. Was it warm in here?

He dropped down, holding his weight on his right forearm, using the fingers on his left hand to peel open the buttons of her blouse. "I'm going to love undoing you."

He tugged the shirt from her skirt and shoved the material aside. Then he unclipped the front clasp on her bra, and pushed the cups free of her breasts.

"You're not wasting any time," she noted, trying for an air of amusement.

He shook his head. "No time to waste. Wouldn't want to get caught."

"But…" Nope, not going to stop him. He might be inclined to slow down to a crawl. Tonight was about the moment. No past, no future, just right now.

He covered one breast with his mouth and lapped at her nipple. He used his free hand to play with the other one, circling the tip of his finger round her areola, bringing up all the tiny bumps and sending a chorus of shivers dancing under her skin. He sucked the achy tip between his lips, flicking his tongue over the top. She'd never realized how sensitive her nipples were. She arched into his touch, encouraging a rougher hand. He obliged by giving it a tug and a gentle twist.

Lena rolled her head to the side and moaned. "Gage. Please,

touch me." She needed to feel his fingers on her lower body. She wanted him to fill her up.

"In a hurry?"

"Yes." She needed to forget about Santo. She needed to escape and get lost in a more pleasurable feeling. She hadn't forgotten the orgasm Gage had gifted her with that morning. Just the reminder made her hungry for another. Maybe that's why he was here now; she'd been sending out vibes, luring him in without either of their knowledge.

Gage released her nipple with a soft pop and raised his head. He stared at her, his eyes hooded, his cheeks flushed, his lips slightly swollen and deeper in color than normal. He was pretty freaking hot. Not a man her father would approve of for a variety of reasons, but she certainly did, for those very same reasons.

He slipped his hand into the waistband of her skirt and dipped a finger into her belly button. Then, splaying his hand across her lower stomach, he swiveled it around so his fingers pointed south and smoothed his palm along her flesh, sliding a finger under the elastic of her panties and continuing on his journey until he cupped her intimately. "Is this what you want?" He grinned, teasing her.

He was what she needed. He slipped one long finger between her folds and stroked it up and down in a delicious and tantalizing technique. "Or is this want you want?" His smirk widened as he circled her clit with the pad of his thumb. Round and round he went, hypnotizing her with his touch and his playful expression. "Or maybe, it's this." He plunged one finger deep inside her, and pumped it in and out, slow and steady.

Combined with the unending stimulation on her clit, her

climax rose fast, coiling quickly for an explosive release. She lifted her hips, receptive and eager for his specific kind of torment.

"You're sucking my finger deep, Lena. I wonder how good you'd feel gripping my cock in your tight pussy."

She panted, but cleared her lust filled vision long enough to peer into his gorgeous face. "Maybe we should find out," she purred.

The widening of his eyes and his swift intake of breath sent a surge of excitement through her. She held her own breath as he lifted away from her and stood, taking a few steps away from the bed.

"Take off your clothes."

She shivered at the erotic promise in his demand. She slid off the bed and stood face to face with him. With their eyes locked to each other's as they undressed, one item of clothing at time, in one continuous heated glance, never wavering, the flicker burning brighter as each layer peeled away.

Naked, and feeling like a low-burning flame stroked over her flesh in a sensual dance, Lena stepped forward, her gaze roaming over his muscular frame. He had scars, a few of them, though most appeared to be old. Each one of them added to the sex appeal he wore like a comfortable piece of clothing.

He had a smattering of light hair on his chest. Enough to tickle her cheeks if she rubbed her face against it. His nipples, perfect dark brown discs called to her as lickable treats.

Gage's thighs were as muscled as his arms. His cock hung heavy and thick between his legs. Her mouth watered. He watched her, his scrutiny penetrating and hungry.

Lena fell as gracefully as she could to her knees. She inhaled his musky scent, letting it saturate her senses. She reached up and wrapped her fingers around his length, surprised at the heat singeing her palm. A bead of liquid beaded at the top, tempting her.

Above her, Gage groaned.

She licked her lips, smiling.

Reaching out with the tip of her tongue, Lena captured that droplet and swept it into her mouth, savoring it for a moment before she swallowed. Then she treated his erection to a swipe of her tongue from root to tip. She repeated the action a few more times until she tired of playing with him and decided to go for the kill.

Rising up on her knees, she lowered over him, taking his cock into her mouth, inch by inch until she reached the point of uncomfortable and ready to gag. Then she backed off, freeing him slowly until only the head remained. She wrapped her lips around him, nibbled on the rim and teased the tiny slit. She swallowed him down again, working her tongue along his length, grazing him with the very edge of her teeth.

Lena lay her hands on his thighs, thrilled when they trembled beneath her touch.

He moved his hips, thrusting forward in short bursts, urging her to take more.

She delighted in his enthusiasm, feeling her own arousal build along with his. Moisture gathered between her thighs and her nipples pebbled to hard points. With one hand wrapped around him, she reached her other down to touch herself.

Gage gripped the side of her head, his fingers twining into

hair, the tug and sting on her scalp shot shards of erotic pleasure down her spine.

"Fuck, Lena, that feels good. But you need to stop."

She paused long enough to raise her head and stare up at him. "Why?"

One corner of his mouth quirked up, then the full gleam of his smile appeared. "Because although the sight of you down there will give me wet dreams for months, I think it would be a shame to waste an opportunity to bury myself balls deep in your body."

She swayed as a shiver claimed her.

"I have this desire to feel your pussy squeezing my cock," he continued. "And if you're going to blow my top off, I want to be looking you square in the eyes when it happens."

"Why?" she asked, intrigued beyond reason for this answer.

"Because, sweetheart, you're going to be travelling that same path right along with me."

That shiver intensified.

"I'm going to build you up, ratchet you toward detonation so we're heading in the same direction."

She gulped.

"And I want to feel every quiver, capture every uneven breath, and watch every moment of the experience cross your face as it happens."

How could she argue with that?

Gage released her hair and reached a hand down to help her up.

She placed her palm in his and he tugged, gently pulling her to a standing position. He kissed her, a sweet innocent peck on the lips that she never would have expected from a man like him. Then he cradled her face in his large hands and the simplicity of the pressure against her lips transformed into a wicked, breath-stealing and earth-shattering experience.

She placed her palms to his chest, curled her fingers and scraped her nails down, raking his nipples in her wake.

A low growl rumbled beneath her hands and his grip on her tightened. "Now, Lena. I want you now."

The raspy quality of his words, the harsh pants, and the slight quake in his fingers, indicated he was traversing the edge right along with her.

He placed his hands on her shoulders and turned her around, giving her a nudge toward the bed and a tiny swat on the ass.

She jumped and squeaked but somehow managed to stroll in a sexy strut to the bed. She turned and sat, keeping what she hoped was a sexy vixen look on her face as she eased further onto the bed.

Reaching the center, she gave Gage her best come hither look.

Chapter Twelve

GAGE PAUSED AT THE EDGE OF THE BED. THE LADY astounded him. She dressed and behaved like a woman used to the best things in life. But beneath the designer clothes and expensive jewelry lay a sensual and down-to-earth woman. Perhaps not as experienced as she wanted him to believe, but willing to take a chance on him for some reason. A reason he had no inclination of questioning when she lay naked before him, her pussy glistening, breasts plump, and heavy-lidded eyes begging him to come to her.

Gage crawled onto the bed, nudged her legs open, and settled between. With his arms wide and his elbows locked on either side of her head, he straddled her and stared at the sight below him.

She batted her eyelashes. "Don't stop now, Gage."

"I wasn't planning to, honey."

She shifted under him, spreading her legs a little wider.

"Shit," he said as a thought crashed into his brain.

"What?" Panic flashed in her eyes.

"I forgot to put on a condom."

"Do you have one?"

"Of course," he responded. "It's in my wallet."

A look of relief replaced the panic. "I'll wait."

This time he did laugh. He jumped from the bed, retrieved the foil packet from his wallet, ripped it opened and rolled it over his erection.

Properly outfitted, Gage returned to the bed. He hopped

onto it, landing on all fours and straddled Lena again, sending her into the cutest fit of giggles. Since when did a giggling female become cute? He watched her for a moment, startled by the sound. She never giggled. Not in his presence anyway.

Gage crashed his mouth down on top of hers.

She moaned and wrapped her arms around his neck tugging until he dropped down flush against her, those sexy erect nipples scraping against his chest.

He lowered his elbows to the bed, trying to keep most of his weight off her.

She angled her head, deepening the kiss, sucking his tongue into her mouth.

Christ she kissed good. She smelled fantastic and her taste was nourishment to his body. He worried that once he was inside her, he'd never want to leave.

Gage shifted positions. He tapped her right leg with his, and she widened further. He canted his hips and the head of his cock grazed her entrance, her heat a siren's call he eagerly answered. He pressed just inside and paused. He dropped his chin and looked down.

Lena stared up at him, her eyes round and bright.

Keeping her in his sights, locked so neither of them risked even blinking, Gage filled her one incredibly slow inch at a time.

Her lips parted. Her eyes darkened and a shudder worked its way through her body.

Gage withdrew at the same speed he'd entered her, and then plunged deep where he stopped again. He dragged a breath deep into his lungs and repeated the move, torturing both of them in the process.

She moaned.

He grunted and began fucking her in earnest.

Lena picked up his rhythm immediately, meeting him at every thrust. Her fingers gripped his biceps. With her head back, her neck arched, and her pulse pounding beneath the skin, she wrapped her legs around his waist and dug her heels into his backside.

Slipping an arm under one of her thighs, he pushed her leg up and pressed it to her chest, spreading her wide, allowing him to sink deeper, her body clutching him like a too-small glove.

His eyes rolled back in his head as he groaned. His skin tickled where sweat rolled down the side of his face. He lengthened his strokes but slowed his pace.

"This is it, Lena. It's time." He refocused, not wanted to miss a moment.

She nodded.

"I want you to keep your eyes on me. No closing them."

She shook her head, sweat holding strands of her hair captive against her cheeks.

"Ready?"

She nodded. She licked her lips. Her lashes dipped a smidgeon lower, but she kept her gaze trained on him.

Gage increased his tempo in increments until he was pounding into her. Wet flesh slapped against wet flesh. Her breathing transformed into harsh pants. Her nails felt like they broke the skin on his arms, but he barely noticed the sting. His cock felt tight, ready to explode. The base of his spine tingled and his balls drew up snug to his body. God damn it. Had it ever felt this good before?

His orgasm began its climb. Energy zinged through his body. Sensation overwhelmed him but he zeroed in on their panting breaths, the moist slip and slide of their bodies, his grunts and her whimpers. It was as though a bubble had formed around them, blocking out unnecessary sounds and amplifying the important ones.

He couldn't tear his gaze away. She was stunning to watch as she fell apart around him. Rather than vocalize her release, her mouth opened, but no sound escaped.

She rolled her shoulders back flat to the mattress and bucked beneath him until they fell out of sync, but it no longer mattered. They were too close to the threshold, ready to jump over that line. They only needed a push to take that final step.

Gage shoved.

Letting her leg fall from his grasp, he slipped one hand between them and brushed his finger over her clit at the same moment he rammed into her body. Lena's release washed over her, drenching him as his own orgasm shot like a rocket through his body.

Gage's body shook with the force of each pull and jerk. Lena's body trembled as each wave overwhelmed her.

Finally depleted, he collapsed, catching himself at the last second before crushing her.

Heavy pants fell from her lips. Her grasp on his arms weakened and eventually dropped away, falling as lazy limbs to the surface of the bed. "Damn, Gage."

He raised his weary head. It wasn't easy. "What?"

She'd closed her eyes, but opened one. "You're good."

He hesitated for five full seconds before he snorted and laughed. "You're not so bad yourself."

She chuckled softly. "We should have put a towel down."

"Sorry." Though he wasn't, really.

"Now I'll need to change the bedding before anybody's the wiser."

"Nobody will notice," he said.

"Ew."

"Look at it this way," he added. "Each time you show the house, you can relive the experience." He knew *he* wouldn't need to be in the house to remember every second of his time here.

"We need to leave."

He sighed. She was right. This was the last place they should be.

Gage helped Lena up from the bed. They dressed in silence, and then he helped her switch out the soiled bedding. When he'd questioned why there were extra comforters, she'd explained the stagers had purchased extras for this particular house. A family home, they kept a spare on hand in case kids running through left a mess behind.

Lena rolled the used one into a ball and carried it with her as they did a final walk through of the house before leaving.

Gage led her to the limo, but she surprised him by climbing into the passenger seat rather than the back of the car. Smiling, he got in behind the steering wheel and started the car.

"How come you haven't told me anything about yourself?" Her question seemed loud in the dark interior.

"What do you want to know?"

"I gather you're not close to your family."

He grunted. He checked the mirrors. He did everything but glance in her direction.

"How come?"

He stopped for a red light. "My younger brother was killed a long time ago. I left home not long after that."

She swiveled as much as the seatbelt allowed and looked at him, her face full of compassion. "I'm sorry. What happened?"

"Wrong place, wrong time. He got caught in the crossfire."

"Oh, Gage."

"I was supposed to go to the store, but I was busy, and my brother wanted to drive the car by himself, so he went without me."

She placed a warm hand on his arm. "It wasn't your fault."

Yes, it was.

"What's your favorite kind of music? I told you mine, but you never told me yours."

He appreciated her attempt to lighten the mood. "Classical."

"Really?" She sounded surprised.

"Yes, really. I like all kinds but my preference has always been classical. I played the piano when I was kid. My mother insisted I learn her favorites."

"Huh. I never would have guessed."

Most people didn't.

"Do you still play?"

"Sometimes."

They spent the rest of the trip in silence. But she slid her hand across the seat, clasped his fingers in hers, and gave them a little squeeze.

He expected nervousness or embarrassment after their little tryst, but instead she appeared retrospective. She rested her head against the headrest, rolled to the side and watched the scenery pass by.

When he rolled up her driveway and stopped the car, she didn't budge. "Thank you for tonight, Gage."

Gage assessed her for a moment before getting out of the

car. He walked around to her side, and opened her door. Lena glanced up at him, took his offered hand and climbed from the car.

He walked her up the steps and to the front door. He cleared his throat. "Lena, I hope you don't regret what happened tonight."

A pretty smile curved her lips but it didn't quite reach her eyes. "Not at all."

"You're sure?"

She nodded and her smile brightened as she tipped up on her toes and kissed his cheek. "I'm sure. I just have a lot on my mind."

He narrowed his eyes and studied her for a moment.

She shifted her gaze away.

"Anything I can help with?" he asked.

She bit her lip. "I need to think about it a bit more."

That was cryptic and raised all kinds of alarms. "Honey, tell me what's wrong." She shook her head and tried to pull away, but he refused to let her go.

"Family stuff that I need to sleep on."

He didn't believe her, but decided not to push in case she closed up completely.

"Do you?" she asked. "Regret it, I mean?"

"Not one minute." He pulled her close, wrapped his arms around her waist and leaned down. He brushed his lips across hers. Surprisingly, she seemed willing to let him take it further but he kept it gentle, sweeter than the ravenous approach his body hungered for. When she relaxed in his grip, he reluctantly broke the kiss and stepped away.

Her eyes had closed, but now fluttered before she opened them. They were glazed.

He raised one hand and brushed her hair back, tucking it behind her ear. "Good night, Lena."

"Good night, Gage."

They stood there, looking at one another, him watching her closely, her looking oddly sad, before she turned and entered the house.

He listened and waited for her to lock the door.

Shit. He had a feeling this assignment had just gotten much more complicated.

Chapter Thirteen

LENA WANTED TO SCREAM AS SHE THREW YET ANOTHER bouquet of flowers into the trash can.

Over the last couple of weeks, Santo had sent her countless arrangements. She'd initially given them to Mary, but when they started appearing almost every day and the fragrance had become nauseating, it angered her.

Then there were the gifts—jewelry and clothes. The jewelry, for the most part, was attractive, but the outfits were slinky and more appropriate for a stripper.

The first to arrive she returned, simply stating she couldn't accept them. But after a nasty email from him about her refusal, rather than confront him—because clearly he had no interest in listening—she simply packed everything into a box and shoved it to the back of her closet.

More worrisome than the gifts, was the paranoia that somebody was watching her. She hadn't spotted anybody, but it creeped her out. Was it Santo?

The only bright spot during that same period was Gage.

Whenever Lena stepped out of her home, ready to show a property to one of her clients, and desperate to wipe Santo from her mind, she found Gage waiting for her, ready to take her wherever she wanted to go.

She loved spending time with him. They bonded during those drives. She discovered she truly liked him. Which made her feel guilty. The clock continued ticking. Yet she found herself hesitant to push Gage into something he wouldn't want.

While in the car, he'd pepper her with questions, curious about her mother and extended family, but seemed particularly interested in her relationship with her father and her own knowledge of the investment business.

He'd gone quiet when she said she had no family members other than her father, and that she had only very faint and often imagined memories of her mother.

He'd been amused when she told him why she'd decided to go into real estate rather than pursue her psychology degree. Didn't most agents simply love to wander through empty homes, seeing how other people lived and imaging their lives intertwined with the owners? Apparently not.

For all they talked, he never indulged her with details of his life. She knew he was estranged from his family and understood the reason. Sort of. Wouldn't you want to be near your loved ones at a time like that?

He'd mentioned college, but didn't say what he majored in, or where he went to school. For a man who managed to pull all kinds of information from her, he was as impenetrable as a rock.

But he looked delicious in a fitted uniform.

And he played the piano like a professional concert pianist. When he'd admitted he liked classical music and had learned to play as a child, she'd thought it cute. Then last night he'd played for her.

That had been a pleasant surprise and a total turn on. They'd gone to his home, where he'd made her dinner. Nothing special, just baked chicken and salad. Then she'd sat on the bench next to him, and watched as his fingers flew over the keyboard in a sensual dance. She'd been spellbound. Here was this sexy, muscled man who made the keys on his piano sing as he played Moonlight Sonata for her.

They'd made love on the floor, an echo of the notes still hanging in the air.

It had been utterly exquisite.

Gage also paid attention. After a chaste kiss when he'd dropped her off back at home, he'd met her in the foyer this morning with a cup of her favorite coffee. She'd told him about a shop near her father's office building where the baristas made the best morning wake-me-up.

"Your father said you had a showing this morning," he commented as he handed her the cup and opened the car door for her.

She smiled. "I do. I don't generally schedule morning showings, but my clients are moving to the city and are only here for a few days, so they're packing in as many viewings as possible." Settled on the seat, she looked up at him standing between her and the car door, blocking the sun from piercing her eyes. "I have a busy day. I had planned on taking my own car today."

"No worries. Your father is working until late tonight, so I have the day free to chauffeur you and your clients around."

"What?"

"I figure it will be easier to let me do the driving and you guys can talk specifics."

She had to admit, it would be more convenient. She could simply give Gage the addresses of the various homes she intended to show. "Okay."

He grinned, leaned down, and kissed her. But he pulled away too soon, slammed the door shut while she sat there a little stunned, and then walked around and climbed behind the wheel.

Lena gave him the address of the first home where she was meeting her clients. From there, she'd spent the remainder of the day showing her prospective buyers three properties. Between locations, they discussed the pros and cons of each, comparables and pricing. Gage remained quiet, simply being the driver, which had initially thrown her clients for a loop, but they quickly appreciated the convenience of not having to worry about directions and distractions.

Lena, however, was distracted by the gorgeous, sweet man behind the wheel. She found herself sneaking glances his way at every opportunity. He enthralled her with his concentration and skill, how he managed to focus on everything going on around him, but instantly responded to her when she simply uttered his name.

The only crinkle in the day was another call from the damned wedding planner. That woman called at least once every few days, and so far Lena had put her off. During today's call, the wedding planner got nasty and said she'd be speaking with Mr. Soranno if Lena didn't soon make the time to discuss her very own wedding.

By the end of the day, her clients decided they preferred the second house and Gage took them back for another look. An hour later, their decision made, he dropped them off at their car, and Lena promised to prepare the offer and have it delivered the next morning. She was exhausted but content as far as her job went. Regarding her personal problems, she was beyond frustrated and anxious. Horribly anxious. The deadline was looming.

Spending the day with Gage, even if he was only on the periphery, had been strangely comfortable. His presence had kept her sane during a time when sanity was highly overrated.

"So, are you heading straight home, or would you like to stop for a drink and maybe dinner first?" Gage called out from the front.

"When do you pick up my father?"

"Not for another two and a half hours."

"Oh. Well, if you have no other plans. I'd like that." It would give her a chance to wind down.

"What do you feel like eating?" he asked.

"I'm easy." She ignored his chuckle. "Do you know a decent pizza place nearby?" She snagged his gaze in the mirror, and almost giggled at his expression.

"Pizza? Seriously?"

"I happen to love pizza? Don't you?" she countered.

"Yeah. Doesn't everyone? But the kind of pie I eat is cheesy, meaty and greasy. It doesn't have strange toppings, whole wheat, gluten free crust, or require a knife and fork to eat."

"Sounds perfect. I hate couture pizza."

His deep from the belly laughter did funny things to her insides. "I know just the place then. It will take about thirty minutes to get there."

"That will give me just enough time to prepare the offer for the Brightons."

While Gage navigated the traffic to wherever it was they'd be sharing a pizza, she completed the necessary paperwork for her clients. By the time he was parking the limo, she was hitting send on the email.

Gage opened the door for her. He'd ditched his uniform hat and jacket, and had rolled up his sleeves, projecting a laid back, handsome as hell appeal. He ushered her inside where a hostess seated them immediately. He ordered a beer and she ordered a wine spritzer.

And then they were staring across the table from each other while all around them frazzled-looking wait staff bustled, taking orders, seating diners and delivering meals. The volume intensified threefold and scents of various entrees teased her with garlic, tomato and spices. Parents raised their voices and kids yelled louder to make their point.

Her and Gage made small talk until their waitress left with their order, a classic cheese and pepperoni to share.

"So, congratulations on the sale."

She glanced up, drawn to his eyes, the sharp angle of his nose, the firm slope of his lips. She loved how his brows furrowed together when he was thinking, or how his eyes darkened when he stared at her hungrily. Like now.

She swallowed. A fan would come in handy right about now. "Thank you. That particular house has been on the market for a few months, so they should be able to get a few thousand marked off the asking price."

He smiled, brightening his face and lighting up his eyes. "You like your job," he observed.

Satisfaction curled low in her belly and pride flourished in her soul, though the crushing weight of her situation dampened it. "I do. I love pairing people with the house of their dreams."

"You told me last time you wanted a functional kitchen, a deck and gardens."

"Gardens I created with these two hands." She wiggled her fingers for emphasis.

"No butler's pantry?" He smirked and his eyes gleamed.

She cocked her head and just stared hard at him. "Do you still think I'm a princess?" All this time she hoped he'd been just playing around with her.

He hesitated, then shook his head. A few loose hairs that had settled on his forehead swayed gently with the movement "No. I will admit that I did. Then I got to know you better. But not anymore."

He studied her and she let him, while she sipped her drink.

"Actually, I think you're a lot less formal than the casual bystander may think. But I do picture you in that kitchen whipping up fancy meals."

She laughed, liking his revised assessment of her. "Actually, I can't boil water so if I could steal Mary away from my father, I'd do it in a heartbeat."

He joined in her laughter. "Then why the kitchen?" he asked.

She shrugged one shoulder and twirled a napkin on the table with her finger. "One of the few memories I have of my mother is watching her bake cookies or make a cake. I'd sit on a stool at the counter and she'd let me dip my finger into the icing or steal a tiny bit of dough."

He reached across the table and took her hand.

She looked down at their fingers entwined and pain sliced through her. She shrugged the melancholy feeling away before it could take root. "My mother's been gone a very long time and I honestly don't even know what my life would be like if she were still around. I'd like to think it would be drastically different than it is today, but I can't say that for certain. I do know my parents were in love." If her father had loved her mother so much, why was he being so peculiar about this marriage thing? "But I can only see that from the few pictures I have of them together."

Thankfully, the waitress appeared with their pizza. After

she placed it on the table between them and refreshed their drinks, they focused on food rather than conversation.

"Any thoughts of settling down and having your own family?"

She'd just bitten the hot pizza and it promptly lodged itself in her throat. After an embarrassing moment of choking it down and then following it with a long gulp from her water glass, she tried another bite. Couldn't answer if her mouth was full.

"I take it you don't have plans to wed," he pushed.

"Ah...well, I haven't ruled it out." She switched drinks, this time taking a decent sized swallow of her wine spritzer. "What about you?"

"I guess I'm not opposed to it. I haven't given it a whole lot of consideration though. Besides, I haven't found the right woman...yet."

"Do you think you'd, ah, prefer a long engagement, or a short one?" Might as well test the water.

"Depends. I'm a firm believer that if it's right, it's right"

Could she make it feel so right that he'd be willing to book a tux in the next few days? "Do you see yourself planning a big wedding, or a weekend quickie?"

He gave her a strange look. "You sound like you're completing a survey."

"I'm just curious." She was taking mental notes.

"Well, I've never pictured a church, hall and half a dozen attendees, so I guess something simple would be my first choice."

And now the biggie. "Do you believe in love at first sight?"

"Maybe lust at first sight. But love? I think that takes at least a few days." He grinned.

He thought she was joking.

"Why all the wedding questions? You planning on asking me to marry you?"

She choked for the second time.

He jumped up and pounded her on the back.

She took another sip of water and wiped tears from her cheeks. "Thank you."

"You going to live?" he teased.

She nodded. At least for the next couple of weeks.

Beyond that, well, who knew?

Chapter Fourteen

"VINCENT, THE WEDDING PLANNER HAS BEEN TRYING to contact your daughter, but she hasn't returned any of the calls." Giovanni glanced at his fingernails. Time for a manicure.

Across from him, Vincent paled.

Giovanni preferred late night meetings. Fewer people around to stick their noses in business not belonging to them, creating lose ends he felt compelled to tie off. Unfortunately, his last meeting with Vincent had to be cut short before he'd even ventured from the car because his driver had noticed somebody lurking in the shadows of the alley.

Vincent fidgeted and played with the pen in his hand. His gaze darted about the room but never settled in one place for more than a few seconds. "She's been busy with work. That's all."

"Have you told her she will be quitting her job?" Giovanni asked.

Vincent's head shot up. "What? Why would she need to quit her job?"

"Because she'll be married to my son. *That* will be her job." Knowing his son, the task she'd be facing was more onerous than traipsing people through other people's homes. "He will be her priority."

"But—"A drop of sweat trickled down the side of Vincent's face. "She enjoys her work, and it will give her something to do."

"She'll have plenty to do." Keeping Santo occupied long enough to keep his mind off the family business would be a full time job. "And once she starts having babies, she'll need to stay home anyway. She might as well get used to the idea." God knew why Santo wanted to have children. It's not as if he actually liked them, but for some strange reason, his son couldn't shut up about keeping his future wife barefoot and pregnant.

"Babies? Surely, you don't expect them to begin a family immediately. They'll need time to adjust to married life. They'll need to get to know one another, do couple things."

Poor Vincent was turning greener by the minute. The level of concern he showed over his daughter's welfare was worrisome. Giovanni could let it slide for now, and play the compassionate father-in-law. As soon as the vows were stated, Vincent would be lucky to see his daughter again. Nothing kept a man in line better than the threat against a loved one.

"Of course I want grandchildren. Don't you?" He gave Vincent the smile he'd perfected years ago to put people at ease. "Can't you see little Angelena look-alikes running around?" Not that he'd ever see any of them. Angelena would be lucky to make it through the first year of her marriage. His son was nothing if not...difficult...on women.

Giovanni hoped having one at home would tame his younger son. He needed a break from dealing with his kid's shit and cleaning up his messes. Fuck. He'd had to send him out of the country to cool off after the last fiasco. The only reason he would be able to come home now was because the source of his problem was no longer a problem.

Vincent reclined into his chair, though his posture and his expression didn't appear at ease or even casual.

Giovanni didn't expect it to. Very few people truly relaxed around him. With good reason.

"I hadn't really thought about it," Vincent said. "But neither has my daughter. I'm not even sure she wants children."

"Well, then, lucky for us she won't really have a choice in the matter." He steepled his fingers. "Santo will make those decisions for her." He would insist on it. "Anyway, I'm not only here to discuss the wedding." He watched Vincent closely, gauging his reaction. "I'm diversifying and I will need your expertise."

This perked him up, but there was no excitement in his eyes at gaining more business. In fact, dread filled his expression. "Diversifying? What do you mean? What are you getting into?"

Giovanni waved one finger at his accountant. "Ah, ah, ah. There's no need for you to know all the details until it's necessary. I just need you to work your magic with the revenue that will be generated."

"But I'll need to set up a new account. I'll need to—"

"Vincent, I will give you the information you require when the time comes. In the meantime, you can start looking at options. I just wanted to let you know that I'll need your support. And of course, I'll expect the same level of service and discretion as with our other arrangements."

Vincent's jaw dropped open and hung there for a long moment.

Giovanni checked his watch. It was getting late and he'd grown tired of this conversation. He stood. When the other man scrambled to follow suit, he silently chuckled.

Vincent hurried around his desk, rushing ahead to get to the door and open it.

"I'll have the information you'll need and introduce you to your contact at the reception."

"But—"

Giovanni raised one hand. "No need to worry, my friend. I'll have it all sorted out by then. You just be ready." Giovanni walked across the threshold and then turned back to Vincent. "Oh, and say hello to your beautiful daughter for me. Please, remind her of her upcoming nuptials, and that it's imperative she return the wedding planner's call next time. I'll expect confirmation that they've spoken and the arrangements are finalized by the party." He smiled, knowing it wasn't as charming as his earlier one. "I insist."

Already Vincent was nodding his head, what little gray hair he had left shifting and bobbing with the movement. "I will, Mr. Soranno. I'll call her right away."

He left Vincent standing in the doorway of his office while he strolled to the bank of elevators and pushed the button. He clasped his hands behind his back and waited. Down the hall, Vincent hadn't moved. By the time the elevator arrived and he'd entered it, Giovanni was certain the sweat that had been gathering at Vincent's brow was now streaming in rivulets down either side of his face.

Giovanni turned and leaned against the back wall of the elevator as the doors closed and it began its silent descent. He rubbed at his right temple.

Nothing satisfied him more than a plan coming together.

* * *

"Angelena Bianco?" A young woman's voice, vaguely familiar, came through the line. She sounded unsure, and worried.

"Yes. Who's this?" Lena had been hesitant to answer the phone after so many horrible messages from Santo.

"It's Rosa. Rosa Soranno."

Lena plopped down onto the edge of her bed. "Rosa," she said, relieved to finally connect with her friend. Thankful it wasn't her brother. "I tried calling you back. I left a couple of messages. Wow, it's been years."

"I'm sorry. It wasn't safe."

"Not safe? I don't understand." Last she'd heard, Rosa was working with a humanitarian aid group on the other side of the world.

"I wanted to warn you about Santo," Rosa said.

Lena groaned. "So you've heard about the wedding?"

"My father told me. I'm sorry, Angelena." The girl paused. "Have you heard from him?"

Lena groaned. "He's been sending me flowers and gifts." Angelena glanced toward her closet. And lewd photos, but she wasn't about to mention those to his sister. "I tried to return them, but it only made him angry so now I'm just ignoring them." And him.

"Santo is in town, Angelena. I don't think my father knows he's here. He came home earlier than planned."

Lena sat straight up. "I know. I saw him." She assumed he'd been watching her since that day she saw him. "Where is he now?"

"I'm not certain. He hasn't been to the house," Rosa said. "But you need to stay away from him, Angelena. He's very dangerous."

"But—"

"Look, I'm aware of what our fathers have planned. But you can't go through with it."

The girl certainly had her attention now. "What do you know, Rosa?"

Rosa sighed. In the background, a door closed, soft foot-steps sounded, and then Rosa's voice again. "I know my father coerced yours into agreeing to this marriage. But you can't. He may be my brother, but he is not good. He's evil, Angelena. If you marry him, he won't treat you well. He doesn't treat *anybody* well."

Rosa's last words gave Lena pause. "Has Santo hurt you, Rosa?"

"Let's just say I keep the lights on and my door locked."

Fear for the younger woman rushed through her. Angelena hopped up and paced the floor in front of her bed. "Rosa, if you're scared of him, you need to leave."

"I have nowhere to go," she said with resignation. "But I don't want to see you end up like his other female acquaintances."

A chill swept through her.

"You can't trust him," she continued. "He is not a man you turn your back on. *Ever.*" Another pregnant sigh, followed by a curse. "You were always so nice to me. You didn't have to be. Please, I don't want to see anything happen to you."

Lena didn't deserve the gratitude. She was thankful for Rosa's friendship all those years ago. Even if it only counted during school hours. "What about you?"

Angelena visualized Rosa's defeated shrug. "This is my family."

"Can't you go to your father? Or are you scared of him too?"

"My father may not be a good man either, but he would never hurt me."

"If they're as bad as you're implying, you need to get away," Angelena insisted.

Rosa chuckled, but there wasn't an ounce of humor in it. "Like I said, there is nowhere I could go that either of them wouldn't find me."

"I know a place," Lena blurted.

There was a long silence this time. "Where?"

"My house."

"Now you're the one who can't be serious."

"Your father has never been here, Rosa. Why would they ever think to look for you under my roof?"

"What about your father?"

Yes, what about her father? Was she really considering hiding Rosa? To what end? The girl was old enough to take care of herself. Lena didn't think her own father would say much. What about Giovanni? She couldn't imagine him being too happy to discover his daughter missing and then find her holed up here.

If Rosa was concerned, and feared her own family members, she couldn't stay where she was. If she'd felt the need to warn Lena about Santo, Lena had to return the favor, if only for a short time. Until Rosa found a safe place to stay.

"When he's not working, he's sleeping. We rarely even take meals together anymore. We have plenty of room. He won't even know you're here." Now that the idea was planted, Lena couldn't let it go. If Santo was as horrible as Rosa was implying, and Lena didn't doubt it for a moment, then she couldn't live with herself if something happened to her. "At least until you figure out a longer term solution."

"I'll think about it."

"Think hard because I'm going to send our driver to your house tomorrow to pick you up."

"No!" she shouted into the phone. "You can't do that. If I'm seen leaving with you, then they'll figure it out in no time."

"I won't come. I'll just send Gage. I'll tell him to stay in the car. Hell, I'll tell him to make sure he takes a different car. All you need to do is let me know what time, and I'll send him right over."

Rosa hesitated for so long that Lena assumed she'd say no again. When she finally responded, Rosa surprised her. "Okay."

Relief the size of a wrecking ball slammed into her and Lena collapsed onto the bed. She stared up at the ceiling. "You're doing the right thing, Rosa."

"And what about you, Angelena?"

"What about me?"

"You can't marry my brother."

This time Lena snorted, though hers held no humor either. "Don't worry. I do not intend to marry him. The very last thing I plan to do is carry the last name Soranno. No offense."

Rosa actually laughed. "None taken."

They finalized a few details for the next day and Lena promised to send Gage to pick her up.

After they hung up, she found Mary and told her a friend was coming to stay for a few days, a friend who needed refuge, not a welcome party. Mary didn't question her. Together, they decided on the room at the far end of the hall. It had a full bedroom, sitting area and adjoining bath.

The best part, it was near the back stairs that went down to the kitchen. Her father never went to that end of the house. He'd never know they had a guest staying with them.

Chapter Fifteen

GAGE STILL COULDN'T BELIEVE HE WAS SITTING OUTSIDE Giovanni Soranno's house. They'd tried for months to get access to the place, and here he was, perched right out in the front courtyard, waiting for Soranno's daughter to make an appearance.

Wade twitched like a live wire next to him, itching to get inside so he could scour the place for evidence. "Christ. I can't believe we're this fucking close, Gage." He slammed a fist against the seat. "We need to be in there, not sitting out in this fucking car, ready to play cab driver to some spoiled mafia princess."

Gage raised his brows. "You got something against drivers?"

Wade tossed him a pointed look. "You know what I mean. Besides, you're undercover. That doesn't count."

"We can't barge in there in broad daylight. Lena said the daughter would be out in a few minutes. If she's willingly leaving her father's home, maybe she's somebody we can get information from."

"Did Angelena tell you why this kid's ditching dear old dad?"

Gage shook his head and then resumed his scan of their surroundings. He half-expected Giovanni's security detail to pound on their tinted windows any moment. "No. Just that his daughter didn't agree with some of the things her father was doing, and felt the need to leave."

They'd switched to a boring looking sedan and slapped a local executive taxi decal on the doors. The guards searched the car before allowing them entry, but of course his and Wade's weapons and badges weren't located. Nobody took a second look at the middle console filled with half-empty coffee cups and used tissues balled up in one of the cup holders.

"She didn't define what those things were, I suppose?"

"Of course not." That would have been too simple. Lena knew exactly why this girl was leaving. She just wasn't sharing that information with him.

"Where are we taking her?" Wade asked.

"Back to the Bianco's. Angelena is putting her up in one of their spare bedrooms."

"Won't Vincent become suspicious?"

Gage snorted. "Hardly. That man lives and breathes work. He doesn't notice much else." Including his daughter most days.

The front door to the large, gothic-style home opened and a young woman backed out the door, pulling two black rolling suitcases behind her. She had a purse strap hanging over one shoulder, her long brown hair up in some kind of messy ponytail. And she was going to trip trying to drag those bags down the front stairs.

Both he and Wade jumped from the car. Being on her side, Wade should have reached her first, but when she swung her head around and pinned him with a wide-eyed look, he stumbled to a halt.

Gage punched his friend in the shoulder as he passed him. "Step in glue?" he muttered. "Rosa?" Of course it was, but it never hurt to confirm.

"That would be me." She gave him a timid smile.

The kid was cute. Pretty, he amended. As he got closer, he realized she wasn't as young as he'd thought. With her hair up, no makeup, and wearing short shorts and a tank top, he'd guessed her for a teenager. But she was clearly older than that, probably only a year or two younger than Angelena.

"You must be Gage?" she asked.

"That would be me."

She grinned at his echoing of her words.

"And the guy with his feet caught in gum or something is my friend, Wade."

She gave Wade a once over, her brown eyes narrowing slightly. A blush creeped up her neck and settled in her cheeks. "Hi."

Wade grunted a response, but at least his feet finally became unstuck and he shuffled forward. "Um. Here, let me grab those for you." Wade shoved him out of the way and wrapped his fingers around each bag, effectively snapping them out of Rosa's hands. He practically ran back to the car with them.

What the fuck was up with his partner?

"Why don't you climb in the back of the car? Angelena told me to tell you that she's got a room all ready for you. She's working this morning but should be home by the time we arrive."

He and Rosa watched Wade jam her bags into the car. She wore a funny expression on her face. "That's fine. She mentioned something about dinner tonight. We can talk then."

Maybe he could find a way to stick around the house tonight, be a bug on the wall. See if any details spilled over a glass or two of wine that could help him nail Rosa's father's ass to the wall.

He planned to attach a small listening device to one of her bags before removing them from the trunk. It would only work if any valuable conversations took place in her room, but it was worth a shot. While he kept the women distracted, maybe Wade would have time to plant a couple more in the dining and living rooms.

Gage helped her settle into the back of the car while Wade stood dumbstruck next to it. "Can I get you a drink? There's water and juice in a cooler in the trunk."

Rosa shook her head. "Thank you. I'm fine. If you don't mind, I'd just like to get out of here before my father comes home." She glanced up at him. "Any trouble at the gate?"

"Nothing to worry about. Though I'm not sure how we're going to explain your suitcases."

She scrunched up her nose.

Next to him, he thought he heard Wade groan.

"No problem. I've got it covered. Let's go. "

"Gotcha." After closing the door, Gage turned to his partner. "You okay?"

Wade swallowed and nodded. "Um. Yeah."

"Time to go." Gage shook his head and jogged around the car to the driver's side. "I'd like to get back to the house so Rosa can settle in."

Gage maneuvered the car down the drive to the guard-house and came to a smooth stop when the two security wannabe's stepped in front of the car. When they'd passed through the gates coming in, the taller of the two men had completed his half-assed assessment of them and the car before letting them through, while the shorter one lounged against the wall of the security hut, smoking.

This time, the short guard strode around the car. He puffed

his chest out, and gave the car a look like he'd stepped in dog crap. He had a snarl fixed to his lip.

Gage barely resisted rolling his eyes as he hit the button that lowered the window.

"Pop the trunk."

Gage schooled his expression. "Happy to."

Just as he bent to press the button, Rosa lowered her window in the back and stuck her head out of the car. "Hey, Simon, I've got two big suitcases of clothing to dump at the mission."

Simon bared his teeth at Gage but managed to twist it into a passable smile for Rosa. "You know the drill, Ms. Soranno. All vehicles have to be checked coming and going."

Gage caught her smirk in the side mirror. "Fine by me. It's your time. No cheap or crude comments about my clothing choices though." She ducked back in and raised the window. Then she stuck ear buds into her ears, and with a bored sigh, closed her eyes and leaned her head back against the seat.

Simon strolled to the back of the car. Gage lost sight of him while he checked the bags. He must have been satisfied, but he did spend more than a minute pawing through her things. Finally, he slammed the trunk lid closed and strolled back to Gage. "You're good to go."

Gage simply nodded, put the car into gear, pulled out onto the street, and released a relieved breath. He had to admit, he ached to get inside the house he watched disappear in his rear view mirror.

Once they were a mile or two away, he cast a quick glance at Rosa. Young, fresh faced, bopping her head to whatever music invaded her ears, she looked more like an innocent college kid than a mobsters daughter.

He lowered his voice. "I'll need to check in with Vincent to see when I'm picking him up. I'd really like to be at the house and try to find out if she shares any of her father's secrets with Lena."

Wade snapped to attention. He cast a quick look over his shoulder. "I can do that."

"Do what?"

"Stick around the house while you pick up Vincent." Wade shrugged and glanced out the side window. "If Rosa needs help settling in, I can help her do that. Or I can just hang out. Maybe I'll overhear something."

Gage shot a quick look at his friend. "What the fuck's wrong with you?"

"Nothing. Why?"

"You're acting all weird and shit."

"No I'm not." Though Wade wouldn't look him in the eye.

Chapter Sixteen

LENA KNOCKED ON THE BEDROOM DOOR AT THE END OF the hall. When it opened, she smiled, truly happy to see a friendly face from her past. Rosa backed away so she could enter.

The door closed, they stood for a moment, just staring at one another. Finally, they embraced.

"It's so good to see you, Rosa." Lena reared back. "Let me look at you."

As a child, Rosa had been like many others, plain and not overly noticeable. One of those kids who blended in. She'd been smart and always did well, but braces, baggy clothing, and downcast eyes kept her on the fringes.

She'd grown into a stunning young woman. Dark hair hung in long waves down her back. Her olive complexion accentuated wide, crystal blue eyes and high, elegant cheekbones. She stood maybe five four and had a curvy body men appreciated. "You grew up. You're beautiful."

Rosa snorted. "You're not so bad yourself." She released Lena's hands, turned into the room, and spun in a circle. "Thank you for letting me stay here. You didn't have to do that."

"Yes I did. And it's no trouble. Your family won't think of finding you here. They never knew we were friends at school so they won't connect us."

Lena followed her houseguest over to the sitting area where they settled in matching dark blue wingback chairs, a small table between them.

Wearing a serious face, Rosa absently scratched the fabric on the arm. "You can't marry my brother."

"I'm not planning to."

"He'll do whatever it takes to make sure you walk down that aisle. He's been fixated on you since we were young."

"He's always creeped me out." He still creeped her out.

"He's never been nice. When we were little, he loved to be cruel. He'd rip the heads off my Barbies and lay them out on the pillows on my bed. He'd cut the arms and legs off my dolls. The one time I mentioned I liked a boy, that poor boy got the crap beaten out of him so bad he spent a week in the hospital."

Lena couldn't fathom a brother doing such things to his little sister. "How did you get him to stop? Didn't your parents do anything?"

"My mom was gone by then. My father was always busy with work. When Santo left me a dead squirrel as a gag gift, my older brother finally stepped in and put a stop to it."

Lena couldn't suppress the shudder that rolled through her. This was the man her father wanted her to marry. "I didn't know you had another brother."

Rosa nodded. "Michael."

"Where's he now?"

"Sicily. I haven't seen him for years."

"Is he like Santo?"

Rosa was quiet for so long, Lena had the distinct impression she didn't want to talk about Michael.

"I didn't think so. At least not when we were kids. But after my mom was," Rosa bit her lip. "After she died, he changed. He played the go-between for me with Santo, but he always remained distant emotionally." She shook her head as though dislodging her memories. "Look, our fathers may have agreed to this, but you can't let it happen. You need to tell them no."

Lena sighed. She slipped her feet from her shoes and adjusted herself in the chair so she could curl her legs up. "Believe me, I tried. Papa's not taking no for an answer. And so far, neither is your brother."

"Have you spoken to him again?"

"I've avoided most of his calls, but he leaves me messages. He's still sending me things."

Rosa looked straight at her, her eyes clear, hard, and serious. "Maybe you need to leave town."

"I can't just leave, Rosa. I can't leave my father here." She'd always known Santo was mean. However, if he was truly as dangerous as Rosa said, she was beginning to fear for her father's safety.

Rosa jumped up and paced the room. "Do you know what your father does for mine?"

"He's an investment banker. Your father has many holdings."

Rosa spun around. "I think he's more than that, Angelena. Do you know what my father does?"

That horrible feeling swirled in her gut. Rosa was about to confirm all those rumors, wasn't she? Lena's conscience begged her not to listen so she could continue to live in the state of denial she'd foolishly created. She didn't want to hear it. She didn't want to face the truth.

But she wasn't stupid. She couldn't deny it any longer. She just needed to be smarter than Santo.

Lena rose, slipped her feet back into her shoes and walked to the door. "I need to find Gage. I will let you know when dinner's ready."

"Angelena."

Lena cast Rosa a pleading smile. "Get some rest." She hurried from the room. Once she'd closed the door, she leaned against the wall for support. She felt like the floor was tilting under her feet. Intuition told her the world she'd believed in all this time had been a fake.

She'd been lied to by her father.

Lena pushed away from the wall. She rushed down the hall and practically ran down the stairs. She needed to find Gage. Perhaps he'd take her for a drive, let her mind clear. She may not know a whole lot about him, but at least she could trust him. If she could clear her mind, she could figure out her next steps. She needed help.

Lena stepped out the front door. The car was there but Gage was nowhere in sight. She left the porch and took the path around the side of the house with the thought that maybe he'd decided to sit out back on the stone patio.

She'd been just about to cut across the flagstone and turn the corner at the back of the house when she heard Gage's voice, bringing her to an abrupt stop.

"Yes, Captain. Wade's managed to get cameras and recording devices set up in a few of the most likely places within the offices and the home. We just need to wait until the reception and then we'll have him. I'm sure of it."

Captain? What was going on here? Cautiously, she moved to the corner of the building. She pressed against the cold brick.

"No, sir." Gage paused. "I haven't been able to do that." He paused again.

Angelena didn't hear anybody else talking, so she assumed he must be on the phone.

A man whose voice she didn't recognize spoke. "Tell him we'll send him the recordings as soon as we can get back in the building after the party. But it might take a couple of days."

Gage repeated what the other person had said. "We're confident we'll have the information we need to nail Soranno, Captain. Everything's in place. It's the perfect opportunity."

Soranno? Which Soranno? And how the hell would Gage know either of them?

"I understand, sir. Yes, sir."

Angelena heard a loud sigh, then, "Did he agree?"

"Yeah," Gage mumbled. "But this is our last chance. We're to report back for a new assignment if we're not able to wrap up this one and have him behind bars within a week after the party."

Behind bars? Gage was the police? This didn't make sense. Why would he be driving for a limo service if he worked for the police?

The other man snorted in disgust. "They'll just put two fresh faces on it after all the fucking time we've put in?"

She risked a peek around the edge of the building. The voice belonged to a man just as big and burly and currently just as agitated as Gage.

Gage stood with his back to her, but looked like he was scrubbing his hand over his face. The other man had his hands on his hips. A dark blue baseball hat covered his head and dark mirrored glasses hid his eyes. He paced in front of Gage like a caged animal. Where Gage rocked the hell out of a tailored suit, his friend looked just as bad-ass in faded jeans and a black leather jacket. When he stopped, she couldn't see him any better because Gage blocked her view.

"Any ideas what to do next? Because, I'm not willing to let somebody else take credit for our hard work, Gage."

He'd lied to her for months, pretending to be their driver.

"Me neither. But maybe the women talked and we can get something off the bug I planted on Rosa's suitcase. She's here for a reason. Lena may be oblivious, but I don't for one second believe Soranno's daughter is."

Gage dropped his head and mimicked his friend's stance. "I need to get into the office. He's got to have something in his files or on his computer that will incriminate Soranno. Men like Bianco usually have insurance. They keep it at home, where it's secure and easily accessible. I just haven't been able to get enough time to do a thorough search."

Lena drew back and pressed her spine against the wall of the building. First Rosa and now Gage. It was time to remove the blinders. On some deep, instinctual level, she'd always suspected the truth, but could never bring herself to believe a grain of it. Acknowledging it would have led her down a rabbit hole. Everything she'd known, everything she'd trusted, would have unraveled on the spot. How could she turn against her own father? Her sixth sense had been telling her something wasn't right. But like a fool—or a daughter who loved her father—she'd ignored it.

Lena closed her eyes as betrayal spread through her like a disease. Had everything and everybody been a lie?

"What about his daughter? Are you sure she can't help us?"

Her eyes snapped open. She stepped closer to the corner, straining to hear every sound, word, inflection in Gage's response.

"I don't want to bring Lena into this."

"She's smack in the center of it, Gage. She's probably just as guilty as he is."

Feet scuffled against gravel and one of them grunted.

"Okay. Okay. Fuck man. What is it with her and you?"

"Sorry. Look, I just don't believe she's involved."

"Do you have proof?"

"You know I don't."

"Then how do you know for sure? The lady may be beautiful, but I don't believe she's stupid."

She didn't know whether to thank him for his assessment or not.

"She's the only person close enough to her father to know something," he continued. "After all these years, she *must* have seen or heard something."

All these years? What were they implying? Just because her father had been working for Giovanni for years didn't mean he'd been on the wrong side of the law the entire time. Did it?

"She's not involved, Wade."

"You can't know that, Gage."

"I do." He sounded so certain.

Regardless of the level of deceit and feeling like she'd been used, relief rolled through her. Gage trusted her. She would probably need somebody in her corner if the police planned to accuse her of something.

"You're sleeping with her aren't you?"

She held her breath.

"My relationship with Lena has nothing to do with this."

"Bullshit." The man growled. "How can you say that? If you're screwing her, of course you're going to cover for her."

"I'm not covering for anybody," Gage shot back.

Even Lena cringed at the anger in his voice.

ANNE LANGE

"But you can be damned sure I'm going to get the evidence we need to put Soranno behind bars for the rest of his life."

So much information whirled around inside her head, she only vaguely heard the rest of their conversation. This changed everything. She needed to leave before they discovered her. Lena pushed away from the wall and ran straight into another one.

A better smelling one.

A familiar one.

"Lena? What are you doing here?"

Angelena looked straight up into Gage's face, his expression guarded as he peered down at her. Those eyes and his clean scent did it for her every time. Instant lust washed through her. God, now was not the time, especially considering the secrets he was keeping.

She pasted a smile on her face. "I was just coming to find you."

"Did your father call? Does he need me to pick him up?" His expression held a hint of curiosity and a whole lot of suspicion.

Behind him, his friend seethed. But he remained silent, probably waiting for Gage to make the first move.

"No," she said, brushing her hair away from her eyes, choosing to focus on his hard chest and the pinstriped shirt he wore. Anything to avoid looking directly at him, though now she wanted nothing more than to run her hands up and down his muscular abs, maybe play with his nipples. How could she be turned on at a time like this? "I was thinking about going for a drive, but I've changed my mind."

"You sure? I've got time."

"No. Thanks, but I think I'm going to head up to my room

156

and do some work. I have a few showings tomorrow that I should really prepare for." The quicker she got away from him, the faster she could get her traitorous body under control.

She turned away, but he grabbed her elbow. She dragged her gaze from his hand to his face and licked her lips, drawing his gaze to her mouth. He probably guessed she'd overheard them talking. She needed to think before she confronted him about it.

"How long have you been standing here, Lena?"

She avoided his gaze and focused instead on the hedge at the back of their property. "Like I said, I just came to look for you, but then changed my mind when I remembered my schedule for tomorrow." She glanced at her watch. "I really do need to get going now."

He stared at her, his eyes narrowed. He didn't believe her. "Is your guest all settled in?"

"Yes. Thank you for picking her up." She needed to get away from him before she spat out all the questions she wanted to ask him. Questions about why he lied to her. Was she just part of the job? Did he always sleep with the women he pretended to work for?

"It's my job, Lena."

She shook her head, confused. "What is?"

"To drive you, your father, or your guests."

She stepped back, struggling to ignore the response of her body being within arm's reach of his.

"Lena—"

"I'm sorry, Gage, but I've got work to do."

She spun on her heel, desperate to run, just as desperate to maintain a normal speed that wouldn't garner any additional attention.

Never more anxious to reach her room, as soon as she'd breached the front door, she dashed up the stairs, enclosed herself in her bedroom, and locked the door behind her. In her mad walk away from him, she'd felt Gage's gaze on her back like a laser beam.

As far as she knew, her father had plans to work late tonight. Knowing that, as soon as she finished dinner with Rosa, and Mary left for the night, she'd search her father's office herself.

She needed to prove to Gage, and the people he worked for, that even if Giovanni was a criminal, her father was not.

Chapter Seventeen

WHEN GAGE RANG THE BELL AT ANGELENA'S HOME, HE wasn't quite certain what he'd say to her. He'd been racking his brain trying to come up with some explanation for what she'd overhead. Damn it. He hadn't wanted her to find out that way. Not about her father, and not about him.

The door swung and his breath left his body in a solid swoosh. She stood before him dressed in sweats and a loose hanging cotton shirt advertising her real estate office. Shuttered eyes stared back at him. He dropped his gaze to her pinched lips. She wore not a trace of makeup. He missed the pearls.

"What do you want?"

"Where's your father?" Had she told her father what she overheard?

"In his room. Why?" She glared at him.

"We need to talk."

She took a deep breath and straightened her spine, but at least the anger drained away. "Yes, Gage, we do. But not here."

"Then let's go to my place."

She looked down at her outfit. "Let me just run upstairs and change." She retreated, allowing him to enter. "Wait here." Her gaze slid over to her father's office and back. "I'll only be a few minutes."

She hurried up the stairs, checking over her shoulder every few steps. He felt uncomfortable now, standing in her home, her knowing, or at least suspecting, his reason for being there.

His gaze flitted over to the closed door of Vincent's office just as hers did a moment ago. Did he have time to do a quick scan before she returned? He weighed his options, keeping one eye on the stairs. He'd be quick. It would only take a minute.

She appeared at the top of the steps.

"That was fast," he teased, but she didn't smile in response.

She came down the stairs dressed in a simple, colorful, gypsy-style floral top tucked into jeans and a pair of white sandals. She had a large tote bag over one shoulder. She looked beautiful, but wary. "I said I'd only be a minute. I don't give false information."

Ouch.

He opened the door, held it for her, and engaged the lock before he closed it behind him. Gage followed her down the stairs, disappointed when she headed straight to the back of the limo rather than join him in front.

He wouldn't let her do it. He hadn't planned on this, but whatever had started between them, he wasn't willing to just toss it aside because she'd found out a few things about him. Gage ignored her path and instead opened the passenger door. He said nothing, just stared at her until she relented with a grumble and climbed in. Relieved, he closed his eyes and let out a deep breath. He shut her in the car and hurried around to his side.

They didn't speak on the drive to his house. His few attempts to engage her in conversation ended in silence, so he finally gave up, determined to hash it out later.

Inside his entryway, he dropped his hat and keys on the

table next to the door while she continued to the living room and sat in the chair rather than on the couch were he could have at least settled beside her. She set her purse on the floor next to her feet and folded her hands on her lap.

Fine. She may be determined to start this conversation across from him, but he sure as hell intended to finish it with her nestled beside him. When had he begun to care so much about this woman?

"Tell me the truth, Gage."

He sat on the couch and leaned forward, his elbows on his knees, his hands clasped together. He shouldn't say anything. Technically, he wasn't permitted to. Confessing his reason for being in her father's employ exposed him. If she *was* part of Giovanni's operation, the whole thing would blow up in his face and he'd put himself and his partner at risk, never mind the case itself. Soranno would go free. Again.

But he relied on his gut. Regardless of what his partner thought, Gage's intuition told him to trust his instincts. He didn't believe she was involved with her father or Giovanni's business dealings. It wasn't her style. She had more integrity than that. He hoped.

"I'm a cop, Lena."

"I guessed."

"I'm on an undercover operation. I couldn't tell you the truth." His boss would have his ass for doing so now.

"Are you after my father, Giovanni, or both?"

He closed his eyes. When he opened them, it was to gaze straight into her dark questioning ones. Worry filled them. Fear. But not anger.

"I'm after Soranno." When she released a heavy exhale of relieved breath, the stab of pain that sliced through him, knowing what his next words would bring to her, almost, *almost* halted them on his lips. But she deserved to know the truth. "Your father is not innocent, Lena, not by a long shot. I'm sorry."

She jumped up and paced, her arms wrapped tight around her waist. "He couldn't have known what Giovanni was up to. He wouldn't knowingly do anything wrong or immoral or illegal. "

"Angelena—"

She spun. "Don't. Please don't say it."

"Lena," he said, his tone low, calming, "your father has been working for Giovanni Soranno's organization for over twenty-five years."

She stumbled slightly then regained her footing. "So what? He's an investment banker. He invests rich people's money. Giovanni is rich." Her words rolled off her tongue as though she'd practiced saying them over and over.

"Your father is the accountant for a criminal organization."

She stopped in her tracks. She looked at him, her eyes wide. "He's not an accountant, Gage. He's an—"

"Investment banker, I know." He sighed. "He's more than just a banker, sweetheart. He has been for years." He hated hurting her this way.

"He can't be."

"Giovanni is one of the biggest criminals in the city. He's not typically one of the most dangerous, but that doesn't mean people don't get—" Gage swallowed roughly "—hurt... or worse. He just usually has other people do his dirty work for him."

But not always.

He scrubbed a hand over his face, then placed his hands on

his thighs and pushed up. He crossed the room toward her, stopping when she sidestepped to avoid him. He shoved his hands deep into his pockets to keep from grasping her by the arms and hauling her against his body. He wanted to wrap his arms around her. Hold her close while she discovered some awful truths.

"Giovanni extorts money, he sells drugs to kids and your father washes his proceeds through a string of legitimate businesses."

"How do you know all this? You must not be able to prove it. Otherwise, he would be in jail."

"He killed my brother, Lena."

She gasped.

"My kid brother. Giovanni shot him to make a point."

She visibly struggled at his surprise revelation before she spoke, her voice low. "But I thought you just said he wasn't... Then why isn't he in jail for murder?"

"Because you're right. All we have is circumstantial evidence. I've been on task teams hunting down men like him almost since the day I joined the force. We've picked off a number of the low hanging fruit over the years. But it's the top of the tree I'm after this time." The one who gives the orders and his men followed regardless of the consequences.

"I'm sorry about your brother, Gage." Sympathy lay in her words and in her expression. "My heart breaks for you and your family. But go after Giovanni, then."

"Unfortunately, it rarely works that way. Men like Giovanni have too many people working under them, and they are the ones who end up doing the grunt work. They're the ones who get caught." This time though, this time, he wouldn't rest until the cream of the crop was wearing a jumpsuit and shackles around his hands and feet.

"This time I want the boss. The only way to capture him is to nail him where it hurts the most, his wallet. Most men at his level in the organization are sent away for racketeering and if we're lucky, money laundering."

"And that's where you think my father comes in."

"Yes."

"How can you be so sure?" Her eyes pleading, she looked desperate for any opportunity to shoot holes in his theory.

He couldn't blame her. "He's been working for him for almost as long as you've been on this earth."

Her face, already tight and pale, blanched. "But you still have no *proof*, do you?"

"We will. Soon."

"How? When?"

Gage scratched his head. He turned and walked into the kitchen, suddenly thirsty. Lena followed and stood at the island while he grabbed two bottles of water from the fridge. He offered her one.

After chugging half of his, he set the container on the counter. "We know of a few of his legitimate businesses." One of which happened to be the corner store where his younger brother had been killed. "We've managed to track the transfer of funds from a computer in your father's office to those businesses, as well as to an offshore account." A small one that had just been opened. They knew there had to be others.

"My father's office?" She released a half-sob half-laugh. "My father doesn't use his computer. He hates them. He has an assistant who does that work for him when he's downtown and he does everything at home on paper in ledgers. Maybe she's the one you should be looking into."

She was grasping at straws. Gage shook his head. "We're pretty confident it's your father. We just need to confirm it." He avoided looking into her eyes as he said the next words. "I need to get into his home office and have a look around."

She stilled and stared at him. "You want to search my home?"

"Yes."

"No."

"Lena—"

"No, I—" Her phone rang.

She leaped for her bag, dropped to her knees, and dug through it until she found it. Sitting back on her heels, she put the phone to her ear. "Hello?" She stiffened and whimpered slightly.

Alerted, Gage rounded the kitchen island and crossed the room to join her.

She rubbed her forehead. "You've been watching me, haven't you?"

Gage edged closer.

She rose to a standing position. "Please, don't." She pulled the phone away from her ear and tapped the screen. A strangled moan came from her throat and then the phone was back to her ear. "Listen, I don't care what our fathers agreed to. I have no plans to marry you, now or ever."

What the fuck!

* * *

She'd felt Gage at her back and regardless of the conversation she was having, her body still reacted to his proximity. When he stepped around her so he was in front of her, she tried

165

to turn away, not wanting him to see how badly Santo's call was affecting her. He stopped her with his warm and solid palm on her arm.

Santo wouldn't quit. When she'd gotten home tonight, there'd been another gift waiting. A dress. At least she thought that's what is was supposed to be. It looked more like a tube top, a garish hot pink chunk of spandex covered elastic that he actually expected her to wear.

And there'd been a note attached. *"Can't wait to see you in this hotness, babe. Just remember, no underwear. I want your pussy available to me whenever I want to touch it."*

Santo used the crudest, most vulgar language she'd ever heard. The only thing that topped his words were his pictures. In the bottom of the dress box, she'd found another image of his cock. Only this time, his hand wasn't covering it. She'd thought only teenagers got off on that sort of thing.

"Who are you talking to? Lena, what's wrong?" Gage studied her intently, his eyes narrowed, his gaze scouring her face. His filled with concern.

"Babe, who the hell are you with? Are you with another man?" The sneer in Santo's voice came through loud and clear. Judging by the look in Gage's face, he heard it too.

"It's none of your business." Everything was spiraling out of control and she had no clue how to get off the ride.

"Fucking right it is, bitch!"

She jerked the phone away from her ear.

"You are going to be *my* wife. That means you belong to *me.*"

She turned slightly away from Gage. "Let me make this crystal freaking clear, Santo."

Gage's spine snapped straight.

"Watch your fucking language when you talk to me."

Seriously? He had some nerve. "I don't *belong* to anybody," she said. "*I* decide who I am going to marry. And it sure as hell will not be to you."

"That's where you're wrong, sweet cheeks," he purred.

"I don't—" She was talking to dead air.

Lena hit end and tossed the phone into her bag. She licked her lips, took a few deep breaths and turned around to face Gage.

He was staring at her, a funny look on his face. "Lena?"

She closed her eyes and shook her head. Every ounce of energy drained right out of her. Gage may have lied to her, but he was the police. He was one of the good guys, right? And he was here.

"Santo Soranno." She sighed. "My future husband, if our fathers—and apparently Santo—have their way."

"Say that again?"

Lena flopped down in the chair. She was so tired. She used the heels of her hands to rub her eyes until they ached and her vision was blurry. Might as well tell him the truth. Maybe she could get him to put his cop hat aside and give her some advice. Without including her father going to jail as one of the options. "It would seem my father has agreed to marry me off to Santo Soranno."

"Do you love him?"

She gaped. Was he serious? Did he honestly believe she would go for a man like Santo? "Of course not. I despise him. I'd rather die than marry that man."

"Then why would you say yes?"

"I didn't," she ground out between clenched teeth. She had the urge to scream. "Did you miss the part where I said, my father agreed, not me?"

"Back up and tell me the whole story."

She rolled her eyes and rotated her head, trying to knock out the kinks. A headache began behind her temples. She sat down. "A few weeks ago, my father announced that Santo had asked for my hand in marriage and my father said yes."

"Without asking you?"

"It's called an arranged marriage."

"Those don't happen here." Confusion furrowed his brow line as he sat opposite her on the matching sofa.

"That's what I said."

"You're not actually considering going through with it, are you?" He looked skeptical and she couldn't blame him.

"Absolutely not."

"So why is he calling?"

"Because neither my father nor Santo are taking no for an answer."

His gorgeous body tightened right up, and his face hardened into a mask of determination, or maybe it was anger. It wasn't jealousy, was it? She wasn't quite sure which it was, but anybody facing him right now would be in for a load of hurt.

"So how are you going to convince them that you're not available?" He somehow managed to say that without moving his lips.

His question zeroed in on her original problem, which now seemed rather mundane compared to everything else. "Actually, I had come up with a plan, but I' don't think it would work now." It probably never had any chance of success. Did she really believe a simple piece of paper would have kept Santo away?

"Why's that?"

"Because my ridiculous plan was for me to get married before the deadline. I'd hoped that if I were already married then they'd just back off."

"Deadline?"

"Labor Day weekend. Apparently that's when Santo and I are supposed to be getting married."

"But that's less than two weeks away."

"Now you see my dilemma." Maybe it was time to purchase a ticket to Tahiti. From there, maybe she'd hit Asia. If she just kept moving and stayed in out-of-the-way places, it would make tracking her arduous. He'd give up eventually, wouldn't he?

Gage's forehead scrunched up and his eyebrows dipped into a low V. He was quiet for a while. Long enough for her to draft her travel itinerary in her head, get up to retrieve her bottle of water, and take a much-needed drink. However, something stronger was preferable. Damn. She still had to deal with him being a cop and trying to arrest her father. Santo had horrible timing.

"I'll marry you."

She twisted around fast, barely managing to save her water from tumbling out of her hand and spilling all over the floor. "Excuse me?"

He rose and walked toward her, a determined glint in his eyes. The same look he'd had as he'd nestled between her thighs the other night and proceeded to bring her to two astounding orgasms using just his talented tongue. It seemed so long ago.

"I'll marry you. We can do it this weekend after your father's customer appreciation event. We'll head to the court-house first thing Saturday morning"

"Ah…" This was exactly what she wanted. Moreover, she

didn't have to ask him herself. She didn't have to fall in love with him. *Pretend* love.

No. She'd never had any plans to fall in love. Lust sure. She lusted for him. He was hot. She genuinely liked him. At least she had until she'd discovered he'd been lying to her and planned to arrest her father.

This would never work. Getting married wasn't the solution. It wouldn't stop Santo.

"If we get married, he'll back off and you won't have to go through with this arrangement." He stopped right in front of her, his muscular body hidden behind a tight white cotton shirt and comfortable looking jeans.

She loved him in his uniform, all bulky and impressive. She adored him out of it. She detected a hint of the soap he'd used in the shower. She pictured his naked chest beneath his shirt. The tiny scar she'd found on his left bicep. He'd told her he'd fallen off a swing when he was a child and a sharp stick had punctured his arm.

"It won't work." But oh, how she wished it could.

"Sure it will. He can't undo a legal marriage," he said. Everything she had told herself.

No, but he could hurt Gage. Or her father. He could make their lives miserable. "He'll just continue to send me gifts and pornographic photos, if for no other reason than to torture me."

"Excuse me?"

Oops. Did she say that aloud? Gage standing so close to her was always distracting. She knew this.

"He's sending you things? And pictures? Of what?"

Anger. Definitely anger on his face this time, and in his tone.

"He sent me a bracelet and a dress." If you could call it that. "And flowers, and underwear." If you could call *them* that. "And some photos of his...um...his penis."

What was that noise? There was definitely a rumbling noise centered in his chest.

"You should have told me. You should have called the police."

She raised her chin and cocked her head. "You are the police."

He glowered. "You didn't know that at the time." His gaze swept the room and landed on her bag. "Are they on your phone?"

She rushed forward and grabbed his arm. "I've deleted them."

He relaxed under her hold.

"Gage, let's get back to my father."

"In a minute. Will you marry me, Lena?"

She wanted to laugh at the casual, emotionless way he'd flung the question at her. This had been her intent all along. Now she hesitated. If only those words held true meaning behind them. "Gage—"

"Lena, let's get Santo out of the picture first and then we'll deal with your father."

She paused. "You'll help me find a way to protect him?"

Gage scratched the back of his head. "I can't promise he won't go to jail, honey, but if he'll help us, they'll probably be willing to cut him a deal."

Meaning he might not die in prison. It was her only option. She couldn't do this on her own. "It would only be for as long as it takes to make this arranged marriage thing go away and to make sure my father will be safe," she said.

He frowned. A pained look crossed his face. "Of course. It will probably be the shortest marriage on the books." He laughed, but it sounded forced.

She considered his proposal. "Okay. Thank you. I appreciate your help."

He lifted one shoulder. "What are friends for?"

Yeah, friends. She needed to get off the subject of weddings. "My father…"

He tilted his head and stared down at her. "I'm really sorry, Lena, but if your father is Giovanni's accountant, then he's heavily involved. I can't ignore that. Neither will my superiors. He's broken the law, and I uphold the law. If your father has been manipulating the money and accounts in a criminal organization, then he has to be held responsible."

Could a heart actually break in two? She heard and understood everything Gage said. She didn't disagree with him. But this was her father they were talking about. The only family she had. She couldn't believe her father, who'd raised her after her mother died, would do this. Some small part of her had to believe it wasn't true.

"Giovanni must have forced him somehow."

Gage nodded his head in concession. "Possibly."

"I can't promise he'll help you."

"He needs to if he wants to have any sort of life. If you let me into his office, I'll find something we can use to convince your father his only choice is to help us."

"Let me search my father's office."

Gage was already shaking his head. "You don't know what you're looking for."

"Neither do you," she argued. "Tell me what you think you'll find and I'll look tomorrow. I'll look everywhere. And if I find nothing there, I'll even look in his bedroom." She prayed she'd find nothing in either place.

Gage didn't want to put her at risk. She could see it written all over his face. When he opened his mouth to tell her no, she threw her arm around his neck and yanked his head down to hers, crushing her mouth over his. She poured every emotion she had into that kiss. Every lustful thought she had for Gage, and every ounce of love she had for her father. She had to be the one to do this. She had to be the one to prove to Gage that her father was an innocent man.

Or, she had to be the one to find the evidence that proved he wasn't.

Lena plunged her tongue between his lips, taking the kiss to the next level. Her body responding when his did, arching to press tight to him. Chest to chest. Thigh to thigh. His hands landed on her hips. His pelvis rocked against hers. She wrapped both arms around his shoulders, angled her head and took it even deeper.

Gage groaned into her mouth. He licked over her teeth. She flattened against him, trying to get as close as possible without being inside his clothes.

When Gage began to back off, she let him. When they finally pulled apart, their harsh breathes fluttered over each other.

"I need to do this, Gage," she whispered. "Please."

Chapter Eighteen

GAGE GRABBED TWO BEERS FROM THE REFRIGERATOR AND joined Wade on the back deck. He plopped into one of the soft chairs, and handed one over to his friend, before he opened the other for himself and tossed the twist off cap onto the table.

"Any word from Angelena?" Wade opened his beer and his cap joined Gage's on the table.

"Not since this morning." And it had taken every bit of self-control not to call her or drive over to her house.

After their talk a few nights ago, they'd lain on his bed and he'd held her while she slept. He would have preferred to spend the night making love to her. But she'd had too much on her mind with Santo and her father. Instead, he'd split the time by coming up with ways to hurt Soranno, and wondering what in the world had prompted him to propose.

There was the obvious inherent need to protect her from an asshole. Just the thought of that man putting his hands on her filled him with a driving need to do physical damage.

The marriage idea had popped into his head as soon as she'd put it out there, and with less than a moment of consideration, had jumped right back out through his mouth. The shocking part? He didn't regret it.

Another, surprisingly smaller part of him realized he'd been offered an excellent opportunity to get even closer to Soranno. Being on the inside, he might finally be able to put his hands on the evidence they needed.

Maybe he was the asshole. One minute he actually considered marrying her, and the next he realized the benefit their union could provide. Was it all about the job? What burned a hole in his stomach most was her statement that it would only be a short-term thing.

Although he'd joked about it, the idea of not being married to her didn't sit well either. He'd known *of* her for months. He'd only truly *known* her for weeks. But in that short time, they'd done more talking than making love. He'd never before considered a woman being in his life long-term. Suddenly he wanted that with Lena. Something told him she might be the one. Somehow, he'd have to find a way to turn their solution to a difficult situation into a lifetime opportunity. They needed more time, but since that wasn't an option, they'd deal with the cards dealt.

When she'd woken up, they'd had coffee together and then she'd left.

Not at all happy with the idea of her searching through her father's things on her own, Gage had spent the day working on his motorcycle. Unfortunately, it hadn't calmed him the way it normally did. Not even tinkering on the piano worked.

"Is she still set on sneaking into her father's study?"

"Yup." He sucked down a third of his beer. After she'd fallen asleep last night, he'd called Wade with an update. He told his partner that they'd been outed and that Lena had plans to search through her father's things. On her own. He hadn't mentioned Santo or the wedding plans.

"Fuck."

"Yup."

"If Vincent discovers her snooping around…"

That was the problem. They didn't know what her father

would do. Gage doubted he'd hurt his own flesh and blood. But Vincent Bianco had serious ties to one of the biggest criminals in the city. Giovanni wouldn't think twice about taking Vincent or Lena out if he suspected for one second she was on to him.

Gage was still kicking his own ass about her overhearing his conversation with Wade and their captain. Now he had to keep an eye on her too. Would she tell her father what she knew? Would she tip him off somehow that the police were watching him?

She wanted to protect her father. He got that. However, Vincent was affiliated with a mobster. He laundered money for Soranno. He shouldn't be allowed to get away with that. Gage wouldn't let him get away with it. That money represented the cash Soranno and his men had mooched or coerced out of unsuspecting kids.

It was drug money.

It was blood money.

Gage didn't want to watch any more kids die because they'd bought a high from the wrong man.

"He won't hurt her." He had to believe it. Vincent might be in deep with the mob, but he wasn't a violent or desperate man.

"You don't know that, Gage."

"Yeah I do. He may not seem like the doting father. He certainly doesn't deserve the father of the year award. But I don't believe he'll put her at risk. Not when it comes right down to it. My guess is he's anxious and grasping at straws right now. He'll stop it before things go too far." At least he hoped like hell Vincent wouldn't hang his own daughter out to dry. Lena had been so convinced, desperate to prove to him her father was not the man Gage believed him to be. He didn't know if he wanted to be present when she discovered the truth for herself.

"Well, he may not hurt her intentionally. But if Soranno finds out, he will not have any qualms about dealing with her."

That's what worried Gage the most. Soranno liked to pretend he wasn't a dangerous criminal. He excelled at making people believe he was just a man who had immigrated to the United States and managed to make something of himself.

The man was a dealer and murderer. Plain and simple. He liked power. He wouldn't think twice about killing Lena and her father if he considered them to be in the way of sustaining his operations. He was a smart bastard. He went to great lengths to make his hits look like accidents rather than vengeance. He had a knack for using local gangs to take the blame for his misdeeds. Unless, of course, he needed to make a point.

Like when he'd killed Gage's younger brother.

Innocent bystanders caught in the action.

Giovanni Soranno, walking away unscathed.

He shook his head, trying to clear away his frustration. "Anything back on the surveillance cameras or the bugs?"

Wade shook his head. "Nope. I've looked at three of the five and so far same as last time. I'm waiting for the others. Somebody working in building security must be on the take. I'm convinced of it."

Gage agreed. Each time they'd managed to sneak past security and the admin staff to set up a few cameras and listening devices, their equipment either went missing or was suddenly damaged beyond repair. Somebody inside the building had to be sweeping it daily. "Did you get the alley camera behind the office building?"

"That's one of the two we don't have yet. But I'm betting it's going to be the same as all the others." Wade paused, his beer bottle half way to his mouth. "A black limo pulls in and we see a man leave the car and enter the building, but he's not carrying a damn thing with him. Then the car pulls away. Fuck, we can't even get a good visual of the driver. It comes back and picks him up. Even though we know it has to be Soranno, he never looks up for the camera to catch his face. So, really, we can't positively ID him as the one entering in the building."

Damn it. They needed this done. Now. "We'll catch him this Friday." Two more nights until the reception. They'd decided to hide a couple of men in the building and have them set up surveillance just before the affair started, giving whoever was screwing with their equipment no time to undo their work.

"Have you heard anything more from the captain?"

Gage growled. "Only confirmation that if we don't get something solid by this weekend he's pulling us out, and putting fresh eyes in." There was no fucking way Gage would let that happen. Regardless of how he felt about Lena's plans to search her father's office in the vain attempt to prove his innocence, Gage hoped she'd actually find something he could use to force his boss to keep him in the game.

His gut told him something big was going to happen soon. He wanted it to be on his watch. He needed to be the one to bring down Soranno.

"When is Lena planning on hitting her father's office?" Wade asked.

The sun had set, leaving a chill to overtake the evening. Even in his cut-off sweats and sleeveless tee, Gage didn't mind the cooler air. Welcomed it actually.

Hot air would have reminded him of his and Lena's sweaty bodies, sliding together on the top of his sheets. An image of her sucking his cock deep into her throat, him feeling the squeeze each time she swallowed, blew up inside his head. He closed his eyes. He was hot for her. Boiling. He casually placed his hands in his lap, hiding his instant reaction from his partner.

"She has some work to do first, but she plans to get it done before her father comes home for the night."

"Want me to head over there and keep an eye on the house just in case?"

He nodded. "Yeah." Especially with Santo now in the picture. He wanted to ensure that jerk didn't get anywhere near her.

Even though they seemed to clear the air, Lena still wasn't too pleased with him. She obviously believed in her father's innocence. Gage wasn't wearing familial blinders.

No little girl wanted to learn her father, somebody she'd looked up to her entire life, her only surviving parent, lived his life on the wrong side of the law. Unfortunately, Gage and the police already had the evidence they needed to convict Vincent Bianco. The only reason he wasn't already behind bars was because he was currently of more use to them on the outside.

Wade stood and stretched. "You want to come along?"

"No. I'll need to be ready when Vincent calls me to pick him up. Call me, though, if anything happens. If anybody shows up, let me know immediately and I'll call her and give her the heads up so she can get her ass into the clear." He couldn't live with himself if something happened to her. "And stay out of sight."

"Will do. Later." Wade placed his unfinished drink on the table and then took the stairs from the deck to the grass. He disappeared around the side of the house.

When Gage heard the engine of his partner's car start and then fade away into the night, he stood, grabbed the bottles and wandered back into house.

He sat at his dining room table, where he'd left his laptop on, and the last page he'd been searching still active. He opened it and stared at a surveillance picture of Lena out for dinner with friends. The image had been captured about six months ago. Long before she'd paid any attention to him. But he'd been paying lots of attention to her.

Between him and Wade, they'd been aware of just about every move both she and her father had made for almost a year now. Before them, another team had started the investigation. They'd never seen her alone with either Santo or his father or any of his men.

Her father was a different story. They had pictures of him with Soranno as well as some of Soranno's men. They knew about the private meetings, as well as those conducted during public events. Not one of the photos were incriminating. A man meeting with his client in the office or in a coffee shop, or having a chat through an open car window, in and of itself, wasn't suspicious. There'd been no exchanges. No transfers of funds made immediately following any of those meetings.

They had nothing.

The records of money transfers they did have originated from Vincent's downtown office. Even his computer.

The problem was they couldn't put Vincent in front of the computer.

The rest of the department, and certainly Gage's superiors, didn't believe for one minute in Lena's complete innocence. They might give her the benefit of the doubt that she had no direct knowledge or involvement of the crimes. However, to have lived in that environment and not have seen or heard something, even a small part of a conversation, didn't ring true.

In his heart, Gage didn't believe it either. He'd just come to hold out hope she didn't realize what she'd seen or heard. Perhaps she was a naïve bystander. If that were the case, then he'd do everything in his power to keep her safe.

From her father, from Soranno, and from the police.

Chapter Nineteen

LENA HAD BEEN THROUGH EVERY DRAWER OF HER FATHER'S ancient desk and every file within his matching credenza. She'd found nothing. Not a single thing to indicate he was even working with Giovanni at all.

That's what equally confused and alarmed her.

The very first time she'd met Giovanni, her father had introduced him as a business associate. Although she'd worn blinders for years, she'd heard the gossip.

After her conversation with Rosa, and then overhearing Gage and his partner, and finally her own discussion with Gage, she'd felt her worst fears may come to fruition.

Her heart held out hope that she'd find nothing, that it was all just a big misunderstanding, or a miscommunication. Even a mistake. She'd take a mistaken identity or a false accusation made by the police. They were looking at the wrong man. Just because Soranno *happened* to be one of her father's clients, didn't *have* to mean her father was also dirty. Did it? Please, don't let that be the case.

In the pit of her stomach, deep in her soul, she knew she was making excuses. Didn't every little girl deserve to believe her father could do no wrong?

A tear slid down her cheek.

At first she considered that perhaps her father simply kept that particular file at his office downtown. Then she remembered him once telling her he kept a duplicate file for his major clients at his home office for those times he worked from home, or needed quick access, saving him the arduous trip through traffic just to pick up a bunch of paper.

Unfortunately, the fact that there wasn't one for Mr. Soranno seemed more dubious. Because she knew for a fact, he was one of her father's biggest clients.

She looked around the small room, trying to see what she'd missed. Her gaze landed on the computer sitting on the corner of her father's desk. She'd planned to look there, but she'd been procrastinating because knowing her father, it was the last place he'd put any information. Her father hated computers. Despised them with a passion. He was old school. He didn't understand or trust the technology. She teased him constantly about his lack of interest in learning so he could be on par with the rest of the world.

He'd always steadfastly refused to advance. Said he didn't mind being a dinosaur because relying on technology often lead to complacency and incorrect data. She'd argued that humans made mistakes too, but he insisted he trusted his own skills, preferring to use his brain to figure things out and confirm results.

Nevertheless, she didn't want to leave any stones unturned, so she booted up the computer and waited, her toe tapping the carpeted floor, her fingers tapping on the desk while she contemplated where to look next.

At the sound of the operating system's musical start-up she refocused on the screen only to see an empty box waiting for a password to be filled in. Damn it.

For what felt like a solid five minutes, but was probably only two, she stared at the blue screen, stymied and disappointed. But she wasn't ready to give up.

Needing to start somewhere, she tried her father's

birthday. Didn't work. She tried her birthday. No luck. She hesitated, her fingers hovering over the computer. Would she only get one more attempt? Angelena typed in the date her mother died. Access granted.

She gasped. She found herself facing a screen with only a few icons visible up in the right corner. What held her captive, however, was the image of her mother staring back at her, her eyes lit up, her smile happy, an infant cradled in her arms.

Why? When? She couldn't drag her eyes away from her mom.

Lena blinked fast, dislodging a few tears that she swiped away with the back of her hand. Now wasn't the time. She needed to focus. She clicked a file, just grabbing one at random to make the image of her mother disappear. But it remained vivid in her brain.

Shuddering, she sucked in a deep breath and opened a folder labeled clients. There were numerous files, all named by company or individual. She scanned the list. Nothing under Soranno, Giovanni, S, G, or any logical combination of his name. Did he use a company name? She racked her brain trying to recall if she'd ever heard one mentioned. Coming up empty, and considering the volume of files she faced, she decided to only go through them one-by-one as a last resort.

She reversed her steps to look at the other folders and opened random files sifting through a handful of them. For an alleged dinosaur when it came to computers, her father's comprehension of spreadsheets and simple databases was astonishing. Why had he led her to believe he hated technology?

The lighting in the room grew dim, casting shadows into

the corners as the afternoon stretched into early evening. The savory scent of seasoned meat wafted down the hall from the kitchen. Mary would be hunting her down to tell her dinner would soon be ready. Gage was probably on his way to get her father now.

Lena sighed and sat back in her father's old but comfortable office chair. Memories of a time when her mother was still alive, when her father truly was her Papa, filtered through her mind. She used to sneak into his office while he worked and play with her dolls by his feet. Sometimes she'd crawl into his lap and he'd give her a piece of paper to draw and color on while he read some report with lots of numbers of it.

She rarely thought of those days. Thinking about them was too painful because not long after, her mother died, and there were no more cuddles in her Papa's lap. No more coloring or playing by his feet while he worked. No more smiles that reached his eyes.

Shaking away the nostalgia, she refocused. She was beginning to both rejoice and fear over the fact there seemed to be nothing to find other than to confirm her father did indeed understand how to operate a computer and she was confused as to why he wouldn't admit to such a thing.

She closed out the file folder she'd been skimming through as her gaze swept over the desktop once again and she fought to avoid locking in on her mother's face. She paused on a lone file labeled JS. Purely out of curiosity she clicked on it, not expecting anything significant since all the other files were typical financial spreadsheets showing investments made, and how they performed on an annual basis.

As she scanned the information on that first page, her

heart thumped inside her chest. Words jumped out at her: *cleaned, safe, undetectable, multiple transfers required, offshore accounts, JS*. And down in the far corner of the sheet, in very small font—*John Soranno*.

Oh God. On the second page, there were hyperlinks to spreadsheets, all labeled with what appeared to be account numbers.

The mouse hovered over the top link. Lena blocked out all other sounds, sights, smells and zeroed in on that one blue line, her determination to find out the truth wavering. Finally, she pressed the mouse button and closed her eyes waiting for the file to load.

She listened to the computer chug along.

She counted to ten.

Then to twenty.

She went to thirty.

The file would be open by now.

She counted to forty, and then to fifty.

She stopped counting, ready to face the facts.

Taking a fortifying, but shaky breath, she opened her eyes.

Numbers. Numbers and dates. Dates and dollar figures. Lines of transactions with large dollar figures. Lots of them. Some dated back to the year before her mother died.

Oh, Papa. What have you done?

Over the next hour, Lena scanned files. There were too many and not enough time to search in depth through each of them, but the few she did spend time on created a sick feeling in the pit of her stomach.

Each file contained rows of transactions; money put in and moved around over the years. She traced dollar figures through what appeared to be tracking numbers. She found original amounts and followed the accounts and values, confirming each had been divided and transferred into multiple businesses. Then split again, and again until eventually it all converged into an offshore account. The amounts varied. The larger the original investment, the more transactions were needed.

The balances in the handful of offshore accounts varied as well. Some would be considered a nice little retirement nest egg for a modest family. While others could help finance a small island. Combined, the sum would be staggering. She refused to do the math.

Disappointment rolled over her. By the time she'd finished her search and printed some of the sheets as proof of her find, she was mentally and emotionally exhausted. She copied everything to a spare thumb drive. After everything she'd already discovered, the fact that her father kept a stash of drives shouldn't have surprised her, but for some reason it did. She'd opened a desk drawer and found a stash of them tucked under a stack of plain manila envelopes. Unopened packages of them. Clearly, her father felt the need to back up his work.

Lena grabbed one of the packages and ripped it open. She slipped the drive into the pocket of her trousers and picked up the pages she'd printed. Then, she closed everything on the computer and erased the browsing history.

With one final glance at her mother's image, her hand pressed to the screen next to her mom's cheek, Lena shut the thing off.

She walked calmly from her father's office, up the stairs to her room, closed the door, locked it, and threw herself across her bed. She could no longer contain the tears.

HER CHOICE

Lena sobbed into her down comforter.

Chapter Twenty

HER RINGING CELL PHONE WOKE HER. ANGELENA ROLLED to her back, papers crinkling under her hip, and rubbed her sore, dry eyes. Her head pounded. Before she could answer, the ringing stopped.

Pulling herself to a sitting position, she cupped her forehead in one hand. Disoriented she glanced around her room. She must have missed dinner. A swath of moonlight cut across her bedroom floor and slipped under her door.

The house was quiet. Mary would have left for the day. Her father had probably come home and retired as well. Thinking of her father reminded her of why she was in her current state. A raspy sob escaped. How could she look him in the face after knowing what he'd been doing all these years?

The phone rang again.

She glanced at her night table and the display screen. Gage. No longer could she hide behind denial. No longer could she make excuses. What would he do with the information? How could they expect her to turn in her own father?

Lena looked over at the printed pages she'd dropped on the bed. She slipped her hand into her pocket and wrapped her fingers around the thumb drive. She pulled it out and looked at it. A tiny device. A whole world of heartache. Years behind bars.

How could she not hand over the proof of her father's crimes to the authorities? If she kept the information to herself, she could be charged with impeding an investigation.

Her father would definitely go to jail. Would they think she was involved?

This was all Giovanni Soranno's fault. He must have coerced her father into it. A man like him would need a man with her father's knowledge on his payroll. Giovanni deserved to pay for his crimes, for forcing her father to do his dirty work. She needed to find a lawyer. She needed to talk to her father and convince him to do the right thing. If he turned himself in, they might show leniency.

The phone started ringing for a third time. She leaned over and picked it up. "Hello?"

"Lena, where are you? I've been trying to call you." Gage's fear and anxiety echoed through the line loud and clear.

"I'm fine. I feel asleep."

"Are you okay?"

"Um...yes." No. So not okay.

"Sweetheart, you don't sound fine. Did you find something?" Excitement entered his voice. Of course he'd be excited. This information gave him exactly what he wanted.

Should she tell him? She needed to tell somebody. She needed help to figure out how to fix all of this. Could she trust Gage to help her, or would he simply focus on his case? Would putting her father behind bars be his priority? Would he care about her at all? "Gage, I think we need to talk."

He paused, the anticipation thick.

She could tell he wanted to ask for details. Guessing she'd found something but not knowing had to be killing him. His instincts had to be warning him. But he didn't press for more.

"I'll come get you."

"That would be best."

"I'll be there inside of thirty minutes."

"I'll be waiting." She disconnected and dropped her phone to the bed, her gaze sweeping over the loose pages. Pieces of paper that contained information that would send her father to jail for helping Giovanni Soranno hide the money he made through illegal means.

She closed her eyes. She needed to think. There had to be some way she could hand Giovanni over to Gage without implicating her father. She couldn't let her father take all the blame. Whatever he'd done, he had to have been doing for a good reason. Her father was not a bad man. He wasn't. She didn't believe that. She couldn't.

She wouldn't.

There was a soft knock at her bedroom door.

"Angelena? It's me, Rosa." Rosa's loud whisper beckoned.

Lena shoved the thumb drive in her pocked and picked up the papers. She rolled off her bed and grabbed her purse from its spot on the floor next to her dresser. As she crossed to the door, she dropped the pages into her handbag and settled it on her shoulder.

She paused at the door, collected herself, and then opened it, the best smile she could muster on her face. "Hi, Rosa. Have you settled in okay?"

The younger woman nodded. "Yes, thank you. Mary is very kind. She's made me feel very welcomed."

"I'm glad." Angelena stepped into the hallway, closing her bedroom door behind her.

"Are you okay?" Rosa peered at her with concern.

"I'm fine. I just need to go out for a while."

"Oh." She frowned. "Work?"

Lena didn't know if she should say anything or not. Then again, Rosa had a right to know what her father was involved in. "Rosa. I found some information today. Some very important information that implicates your father," she swallowed hard "and mine in possible criminal activity."

Rosa blushed and dropped her gaze.

She knew. Rosa knew all about her father. "How come you never said anything?"

"It's not something I'm proud of, Angelena. How exactly does one tell the only person she ever considered a friend that her family is tied to organized crime? Or that she suspects her friend's own father may also be a criminal? It doesn't really make for good relationship building conversation."

Lena didn't know how to respond. Nevertheless, she understood completely. What in the hell were they going to do about their fathers? "I need to go."

"Do you want me to leave?" Rosa's lower lip trembled just the slightest bit.

"No, not at all. We'll figure this out." Somehow. She had no clue how, though.

"Let me help."

"I can't let you do that, Rosa. Not yet anyway. Your father doesn't know you're here. Let's keep it that way for now. If anything happens or is about to happen, I'll let you know. Then you can decide your next steps."

"I don't like it, but I trust you. Promise you'll let me know if you need anything at all."

"I promise." Lena drew Rosa into a brief hug, said good-bye and then hurried away. That young woman's father was a major player in illegal activity. There was no way she'd put Rosa at risk.

Now she needed to convince Gage to help her and her father.

* * *

Gage pulled up to Lena's front door, ready to hop out, but she was already coming down the steps. She opened the door, climbed in and slumped against the cushioned seat looking as defeated as he'd ever seen a person.

"Can we please just drive?" She kept her gaze glued to the passenger side window.

Gage still raged over the fact that her father had arranged a marriage to the spawn of a man like Soranno. Santo was scum, plain and simple. If his father and older brother were the brains behind their organization, Santo was the brawn. At least, he liked to consider himself the heavy in the family. From all accounts, he was nothing more than a common thug.

While he'd been waiting for Lena to call him, he'd done some digging. There wasn't much on the older son, Michael, but there was plenty on Santo. He had been trouble since birth. Years of misdemeanors, charges as a youth and beyond, but every single time, he'd gotten off. Daddy had obviously paved the pathway to freedom.

The thought of Lena spending even one moment in that creep's company twisted his gut. He clenched his fists. There was no way he'd allow her to marry that man. But first things first. "You found something incriminating." He didn't have to ask. He knew from the bleak expression and despondent tone.

"I don't know what to say to you, Gage."

He glanced at her as he drove. "You can tell me anything, Lena."

"No. No I can't. Not this."

He reached across the seat and grasped her hand. "Honey, you need to trust me."

She turned her head. Her eyes, shiny with tears and hopelessness. "Gage…"

"How deeply is your father involved, Lena?"

Tears ran down her cheeks. He reached up, but she batted his hand away and then wrapped her arms around her middle and faced forward.

Gage came to a red light and stopped. He took the opportunity to turn just enough to face her. He grasped her chin in his hand, forcing to her look at him.

"Lena. I'll help your father as much as possible. But, honey, you need to tell me what you found. If I can put Giovanni away, he won't be able to hurt any other people or continue to commit the crimes that he does."

"But you don't know…"

"Yes, Lena, I do. That man hides behind expensive suits and businesses he claims are legitimate. But he's a mobster, sweetheart. He sells drugs to kids on the street. He kills people."

"I found nothing specific about drugs."

"No. But considering your father is a financial wizard, I'd bet you found offshore accounts. Lots of money being funneled from one business or account to another."

She paled and jerked her chin back. The light had turned green, forcing Gage to drive. They said nothing more for a few minutes as he drove through the intersection and searched for a place to pull over. Some place where they could talk without drawing unwanted attention.

Lena slumped in her seat and refused to look in his direction. She must have found the jackpot. Gage's own tension level rose. Maybe, after all these months, he would get the evidence he needed to get Soranno off the streets for good.

Gage drove to the park. There would be plenty of space and plenty of privacy there for them to have this conversation.

He followed the winding drive to the small public parking lot in the back near the man-made pond. Like he'd hoped, there was only one car there. He pulled into an empty space near the end of the graveled area, and as far from the other vehicle as possible. Out of habit, he ensured he had good visibility.

He shut off the engine, turned in his seat and faced Lena. She hadn't uttered a word in the last ten minutes, but each hushed sniffle broke his heart. The moonlight caught her hair, making sections of it appear almost blue. Her washed-out features and red-rimmed eyes told him she'd been suffering for hours. He didn't relish the idea of being the person responsible for sending her father to prison, but in spite of his feelings for her, he had a job to do. Whether it sucked right now or not.

"Okay, Lena. Tell me what you found."

She sighed heavily, her whole body shuddering with the effort. She raised one hand and brushed her hair away from her face.

He admired the steadiness of her hand given the way the rest of her trembled.

"Tell me?" he said softly.

"Everything was on my father's computer under the name of John Soranno."

To say he gaped was an understatement. "You got into your father's computer files?"

She closed her eyes and nodded. She licked her lips, took a deep breath and opened her eyes. She stared straight at him, her determination stark in the tightness of her features. Was the betrayal he saw in her expression for him or her father?

"He had no paper files on hand. At least none that I found. There were file folders for his other clients, but nothing for Giovanni. Frankly, his computer was the last place I looked. I'd almost given up."

"Why?"

"Because my father's a technology dinosaur. He knows nothing about computers, or so I'd thought." She snorted. "Apparently that was a lie too."

"What kind of information did you find?"

Angelena unclipped her seatbelt and swiveled. "Most of it was regular financial spreadsheets tracking various transactions of funds being moved from one location to another. I didn't have time to go in depth, so I only picked a couple of items and followed them through. He's clearly got a number of businesses—"

"Probably most of them are fake."

She waved away his interruption. "Maybe. I don't know. There appeared to be a number of different bank accounts too."

"What about names?" He needed to make sure he could tie everything to Giovanni.

"He used JS for John Soranno. I know Giovanni prefers to be called John when it comes to business."

"Only initials? Nowhere is his name spelled out?" Would the initials alone stick? He needed more.

"Only in one spot. But like I said, I didn't go through everything."

"Are you sure of what you found?" He didn't doubt her. His gut told him the info was sound, but he had to be absolutely positive.

"Yes." She grabbed her purse from the floor, unzipped it and pulled some folded sheets of paper out.

He reached to take them, but she pulled her hand back.

"I printed a few pages off. I don't know if it will mean anything at all, but..." she shrugged and then her shoulders slumped.

"Give me the papers, honey."

A tear slipped from the corner of her eye and travelled down her cheek.

"Please, Lena." Gage held out his hand again.

She handed them over. "The rest of it is on a thumb drive."

He took the papers and unfolded them. He scanned the sheets, but nothing jumped out at him as glaringly implicating. Only Giovanni's name. Then again, he wasn't an investment banker. He hoped it was enough for a warrant. He and Wade could go through them later. His priority tonight was Angelena.

"I'm sorry, sweetheart."

"Me too." She stared down at the potential evidence he held. "What will happen to him, Gage? I don't want to see my father spend the rest of his life behind bars." Another tear rolled down her cheek. She swiped it away angrily.

"If he agrees to help the police and tell them everything he knows, they might be willing to cut a deal for him. I can't promise he won't spend time in jail, sweetheart, but if he cooperates, they might consider reducing the charges."

He didn't want to see her go through this pain. It wasn't her father Gage was after. He wanted the man at the top. Men like Giovanni sat pretty and kept their hands clean. Most of the time. Men like Giovanni normally directed the minions below him to carry out his orders. They let the other people

take the fall, and assume all of the blame while they continued to climb to the top, stepping over anybody who got in
their way. When somebody fell, they simply looked the other
way and hired more groupies to take their place.

Gage held out his hand again, but Lena just looked at him
blankly.

"What?" she asked.

"You said you saved everything to a flash drive. Give it to
me and I'll hand it over to my captain. He'll know what to
do with it."

"No."

"No?" Did he hear her correctly?

"I don't have it."

Gage was confused. "Where is it?"

"In a safe place," she replied.

"Lena."

"I'm not handing everything over to you, Gage. Not until
I've had a chance to talk to my father."

"Lena you can't. If he says anything to Soranno…" He
might as well quit, because he'd be fired for blowing his cover
and the case.

"I need to understand why my father did it. I need to know
before I let anything happen to him."

"I won't let—"

She threw up a hand. "You can't guarantee that. I don't
care about your case, Gage. I do care about my father. I need
to try to convince him to give up the information himself. I
need him to realize he needs to ask for help so he can get out
of whatever trouble he's in."

Gage scrubbed a hand over his face and took a calming
breath. "And if he won't?"

"Then I'll give you the flash drive myself."

"When are you planning on having this father daughter chat?"

"Tomorrow."

Gage looked out the side window. It was late. He could wait one more day. Tomorrow night was the reception. This time Giovanni was not going to get away.

And he deserved every bit of pain and loss coming to him.

Chapter Twenty-One

LENA WALKED PAST HER FATHER'S SURPRISED ADMINISTRA-tive assistant and without even knocking, entered his office.

"Papa, we need to talk."

She stood in front of his desk, hands on her hips. Then she crossed her arms over her chest. Then she just let them rest at her side. She refused to sit for this.

Why couldn't things be different?

"Mr. Bianco, I'm sorry, but your daughter didn't give me a chance to tell her you were busy."

"That's fine, Debra." He waved the middle-aged woman away and waited until she'd closed the office door before he turned his attention back to her. "Angelena, what are you doing here? As you can see, I'm busy."

After she'd spoken with Gage last night, she'd had him drive her straight back home. He'd wanted to take her to his place, but she couldn't spend the night with him. There was too much at stake, including her heart.

She'd woken this morning realizing she needed to deal with this now. She had to try to talk some sense into her father, convince him to turn himself over to the police.

"This is important, Papa."

He fidgeted with a pen on his desk, poised over a document in front of him. "Can't we talk when I get home? I have to finish this report." He picked up a few papers from his desk, probably for effect.

Her gaze jumped to his computer. He had the screen positioned away from her, but the sly glance he gave it confirmed it was turned it on. Funny, in all the years she'd interrupted him when he worked at home, she'd never paid close enough attention to notice. She'd taken his casual comments regarding technology and his lack of interest at face value.

Now she took note of the tension in his body, the slight edge to his smile, the covert peeks at the display screen. "No. We need to talk now."

He gave her a stern look. "Angelena—"

"I know what you've been doing."

His eyes narrowed.

She watched as he worked to figure out what she was talking about.

Then, as though a light went on, his eyes widened as understanding dawned. After a brief flare of panic, he dropped his gaze to his work. "I don't know what you're referring to." He wouldn't look her in the eye.

"I know about Giovanni Soranno."

He glanced up and what looked like relief settled on his face as he laughed, though there was a ring of uncertainty in the sound. "Of course you know Mr. Soranno. He's my client and about to become your father-in-law."

"Over my dead body will that ever happen."

"Angelena," he scoffed, "don't ever say anything like that." He paled.

Was that fear in his eyes?

"I'm not here to talk about a wedding that will never take place. I'm here to talk about the work you do for him, and the fact that you were prepared and willing to marry me off to a criminal."

"What?" He gulped. He blinked rapidly. His gaze darted around the room, too fast to settle in any one place for more than a second.

"Papa, why?" Without warning, a sob caught in her throat and tears gathered in her eyes. Until now she'd been mostly scared and confused, and honestly, still trying to stay heavily in denial mode even though the truth was spread out before her, like some horrible rancid feast. Like any good, devoted daughter, she kept trying to look in another direction. *Any* direction.

Everything had changed, though. In addition to rage at Giovanni for involving her father in his activities, and anger at her father for succumbing to a man like that, hurt unlike any she'd ever felt surged through her.

She'd been saddened when her father first announced this engagement farce, but knowing that he'd agreed to hand her over to a man who led a criminal organization stunned her. How could he do that? He must have known, or at least suspected, what Giovanni might be capable of.

She dropped into the chair opposite him and leaned forward, finally catching and keeping his attention on her face. "I *know*, Papa."

He blinked a few times, and then dropped his gaze. "I don't know what—"

She slammed the palm of her hand on the top of his desk.

Her father flinched in his seat.

"Papa, I know all about the money laundering. I know all about the many, many businesses, most of which I'm sure don't even exist other than perhaps on paper. I know all about the offshore accounts." His gaze flew to the computer. "I know everything."

"Lena, what did you do?" he whispered. Panic saturated every single word he said and breath he took. His face turned ashen. His hands trembled.

"You need to go to the police, Papa. You need to tell them *everything*." He needed to come clean so she wouldn't be forced to do it for him.

He dropped his face into his hands and shook his head. He muttered, "No. No. No."

"Papa, if you help them, they'll be willing to help you."

"No. No. No."

"Papa, they'll make a deal with you. I'm sure of it. We'll get you a good lawyer."

"I can't give them anything, Lena."

"Can't, or won't, Papa?"

He shook his head.

"It's too late," she stated, her voice firm.

His head shot up. "What?"

"I gave them everything they needed." Actually the flash drive was tucked away in the back of her sock drawer. But she had every intention of turning it over to Gage. She just hoped and prayed her father would be standing next to her when she did.

All the tension drained out of her father. It was if somebody had pulled a plug and sucked the life right out of him. One minute he'd been stiff with anxiety and the next, he sagged like a rag doll. His shoulders drooped, all expression on his face fell away, and he sunk two inches in his chair.

"How? When? Why, Lena? Why would you do this to me? To us?" His eyes had gone blank. He looked like an old man sitting in his office chair.

How could she continue to go through with this? She

didn't care what Gage had told her. She didn't care about the promises he had given. There had to be some way she could keep her father out of jail.

What could she do? She couldn't appeal to Gage. He had a job to do and he was an honorable man. No matter what he felt for her, he was compelled to follow the law. She wouldn't ask him to break it.

"Angelena, how did you—"

"I searched your office at home, Papa. Imagine my surprise at discovering how well you actually do know how to use a computer. Quite well I might add."

He blanched. His gaze now swinging to his computer and sticking there.

"I found files for JS. I glanced through them, and it doesn't take an accountant to realize something's not quite right."

He blinked, but didn't respond.

"Papa, why? Why have you been doing this? You're better than that. You're better than *him*."

Now she slumped into the chair. Exhausted. Saddened. Heartbroken. Just broken.

Her father raised his head slowly and looked at her. She didn't recognize the emotion shining in his eyes, but before she could hazard a guess, he blinked, dropped his chin and closed them. A single tear leaked from the corner of one and slid silently down his cheek.

"Papa?" she whispered.

Wounded. Defeated. Resigned. Those were the descriptors that came to mind as she waited for him to talk.

"You were very young when your mother became ill," he began, his voice hollow. "We found out not long after your birth that she had a rare form of cancer. We'd thought we'd caught it early enough to fix it. But we didn't have much money, and the treatments were very expensive."

He swallowed. His eyelashes fluttered rapidly as he battled the tears that continued to seep from his eyes. Any words she might have offered were stuck in her throat.

"When she grew so tired and weak, and then the pain began to get worse, I became desperate. I had been working with a new client. He was wealthy. He had quite a few businesses it seemed. And he took a liking to me. He was pleased with how well I handled his accounts and invested his savings." He glanced up at her. "Especially when I discovered that many of those businesses didn't exist beyond a fake name on a piece of paper and I said nothing about it." The anguish in his face, in his eyes, in his words, dug into her soul and took hold, twisting until she felt it too. "I didn't know what else to do. My wife, the love of my life, was dying. My little girl, my baby was going to grow up without her mother. I didn't know what else to do."

"The bank? What about a loan?" she asked.

He shook his head. "We had no collateral. We had nothing to offer that would return us the kind of money we needed. All the savings we had went into your mother's health. The treatments and medications didn't come cheap."

"Family?"

"My parents were gone by then. Your mother's parents had nothing. It was hard enough telling them that their only daughter had a very limited time left on this earth. We couldn't bring ourselves to ask them for what little they did have."

"When you went away on that vacation…" She paused. "It wasn't a vacation, was it?"

"No. We spent the first three weeks at another hospital. Nothing they tried work. We took the last week and went back to Sicily so your Mama could say goodbye."

"And the hospital bills?" Although she suspected the answer now, she had a perverse need to hear her father say it aloud.

"Piled up. I'd paid everything I could and there were still so many. And then the funeral costs. I didn't realize at the time how expensive it was to bury somebody." He glanced down at his hands. "One of my clients offered to lend me money."

"Giovanni."

Her father nodded. "He'd actually lent me a little before that as well for some of the tests and various treatments. That last round was experimental and very pricey."

"Did Mama know?"

"No. I just told her I'd worked out a payment plan with the hospital."

"How much?" she asked.

"A lot," he replied and tightened his lips.

"Why didn't you just pay him back?" That's what confused her the most. After all these years, surely her father had paid out the loan.

"He wouldn't take the money."

She had no clue how to respond to that one. "I don't understand."

"He didn't want my money."

"But I thought it was a loan."

Her father closed his eyes. When he opened them, the distress he'd managed to put aside while he told her was back full force. "He wanted me to work it off."

She shook her head. "But, then why the marriage arrangement?"

"Apparently that's the interest."

Chapter Twenty-Two

LENA WALKED OUT INTO THE BLAZING SUNLIGHT. How could such a dismal day have such a bright appearance? After her father finished his story, she'd managed to get him to agree to go to the police with her. It hadn't been easy. They'd fought over it for a good thirty minutes. Only when she'd finally broken down and sobbed in his arms, did he relent. But he insisted it be after tonight's customer appreciation event, although he'd argued when she told him she'd attend with him. This might be the last evening she had with her father, and it would be spent with dozens of other people as well, but there was no other place on earth she'd be.

He was frightened, and with good reason. Nobody just walked away from a criminal organization. But she was determined to find a good lawyer. Somebody who would work with them to keep her father out of jail, or at least minimize the time he did need to spend behind bars. Maybe they could put him into witness protection if he agreed to testify. She'd rather that happen than see him behind bars for the rest of his life all because he had to pay off the bills from his dying wife's hospital stays.

She'd have to talk to Gage too. If her father had to go into hiding, she intended to go with him. It would be hard to say goodbye to Gage, but at least he'd have what he wanted, the evidence to put Giovanni Soranno away for a very long time.

Avoiding Gage this morning hadn't been easy. She hadn't wanted him to confront her father. So she'd called another car service and had Mary tell her father Gage was busy, and another driver would be there to take him to work thirty minutes earlier.

She hadn't seen Rosa either and felt guilty about skipping out on her again. But she'd been in a rush to get downtown to talk to a lawyer. Lena paused near the ally midway down the block to where she'd parked her car while a group of tourists strolled by and took pictures.

Suddenly a hand wrapped around her bicep and yanked her back into a hard chest. Another hand covered her mouth, preventing a scream from passing her lips. Somebody pulled her roughly into the alley. She scuttled quickly so she wouldn't stumble and fall. She was horrified that nobody within her vicinity even blinked at a young woman being accosted.

Petrified, she sucked in air through her nose, trying to figure out how to get away from her attacker. When he spun her around and pushed her up against the brick wall, she pulled in every ounce of oxygen she could find, ready to let lose the mother of all screams.

"Angelena. How's my sexy bride-to-be?"

Her eyes focused on the man pressing the length of his body along hers. One of his hands still covered her mouth, his other made its way down her side and over her hip. It's too bad he wasn't a disgusting troll, because that would make it so much easier to believe him capable of the things she now knew he was.

"Are you going to scream if I let you speak?"

She shook her head, very weary of the mean glint in his bedroom eyes.

He removed his hand. His aftershave assaulted her.

She forced back a gag threatening to escape.

Had he found Rosa? Is that why he was here? No. He couldn't have. Nobody would guess where she was.

"I just thought I'd surprise my bride." He grinned.

On most men, a smile like that would be considered sexy, mischievous even. On Santo, it just looked evil. "What do you want?"

She cringed with revulsion when he dipped his head and blew his hot, rancid breath over her ear.

He pulled back and snorted. "Why, to spend some quality time with my soon to be wife, of course." His eyes raked over her and she felt the need for a shower. Maybe two. "Get to know one another better." He cupped her breast and squeezed, not at all gently. "After all, our last visit was cut short."

She slapped his hand away. "Get your hands off me."

His lip curled into a snarl and his eyes narrowed to mean slits. Santo grabbed her by the shoulders and shoved her back against the brick wall. Her head whipped back. She gasped at the onslaught of pain. But the agony at the back of her head was nothing compared to the disgust she felt from the rough grinding of his pelvis in the cleft of her thighs, or his hand squeezing her throat. Or the pull of his fist in her hair.

Her scalp screamed for relief. His beer-laced breath smothered her. She wanted to puke. No. Check that. She wanted to knee him in the balls first, then puke, before she rushed straight home to scrub away the filth of his touch.

"You're gonna be my wife, slut. I can fucking touch you however I want," he whispered fiercely.

Angelena fought to keep the tremble from surfacing. She'd never been so frightened. He wasn't much taller than her, but his grip was stronger, his mood definitely blacker. His dark hair hung low over his cold, empty eyes. He had no soul. All she saw when she looked him in the eye was her own reflection. No that wasn't quite true. She saw evil. And the knowing grin indicated his distinct pleasure at seeing her fear.

"Whenever I want." He glared at her with malicious intent. "Did you like my last gift? You know, I'm still not too pleased you tried to send the first ones back. I bought those special for you, babe. You should be grateful. You should *always* be grateful."

Grateful was the last emotion she'd ever feel in connection with this man.

"I can't wait to see you wearing those clothes. Fuck, babe, you're going to look so hot." He leaned far enough away to scan his slimy gaze down and up her body. He licked his lips and whistled low. "Fuck yeah. I can't wait to watch you strut around in them. Then I'll rip them off this fabulous body of yours and fuck you senseless." He grinned. "How does that sound?"

Like she'd just stepped into hell.

"Who was that man you were with when I called?"

She should have known he wouldn't forget that. "I don't know what you're talking about."

He tightened his grip in her hair. "Yes you do. Don't lie to me."

Tears burned in her eyes. "It was just my father's driver."

"No more men. I don't care who they are. You're gonna be *my* wife."

"But I don't want to marry you, Santo. I don't love you. You don't love me." She had to find a way to reason with him. "Surely you want somebody you love."

He threw back his head and laughed like she'd just told him the funniest joke of all time.

She couldn't help the flinch. The diabolical sound falling from his mouth scared the living hell out of her. This man intended to hurt her. There was no doubt in her mind.

"It ain't got nothing to do with love, sweet cakes," he said, his sick glee at her expense finally contained. "It's got to do with business." He leaned close and sniffed her hair. His tongue snaked out and he licked up the side of her neck.

Oh, God, she really was going to throw up.

"But I will admit, I'm sure looking forward to sticking my cock inside you. I bet you haven't been with too many men."

"I'm twenty-nine, Santo." Most women her age had been with many men. Just not her.

He snorted. "I know how sheltered your daddy has kept you, honey. There can't have been *that* many men." He sneered. "Tell me. You a virgin? I ain't never bagged me a virgin before."

She knew he'd gone to Sunday school as a child and attended well-respected schools. But he behaved as though he'd crawled out from the gutter. And proud of it.

"No. I'm not a virgin."

A fleeting look of disappointment crossed his face, before that sick smile returned. "Well that's good then. I won't have to go easy on you."

She shuddered.

"Ooh. Look at you shake, baby. Hot for me already, are you?" He pressed close, his erection tight to her belly.

Her stomach rolled dangerously.

"I was thinking we should move the date up. So you don't try and find a way to ditch me."

The thought crossed her mind every single day.

"Not gonna happen, babe." He squinted at her obviously reading her mind.

That cold look left her utterly chilled. And scared senseless. This man could hurt her. He *would* hurt her. Or worse.

"You had better be walking down that aisle on our wedding day, bitch. Because if I don't see you there—"

"What?" she whispered. What would he truly do to her if she failed to show? Threaten her? Hit her? Kill her?

"You love your old man don't you?"

"Of course."

"You want him to live long enough to play with your babies, don't you?"

"What?"

He smiled. Not a pretty smile. Not even a trust-me smile. Well, that's not true. It *was* a trust-me smile. Just not a 'trust-me-I've-got-your-back' smile.

"If you aren't dressed in white and joining me at the front of the church on our wedding day—" He leaned close and whispered, "I will kill your father, Angelena."

Bile rose in her throat. Tears swam in her eyes. Her heart thudded in her chest. He wanted to marry her *that* badly? Why? What was so special about her? She couldn't marry Santo. She just couldn't. But would he actually kill her father if she didn't'?

"Santo," she whispered, not sure what she'd say but needing desperately to find the words to put an end to this.

"And I'll make you watch," he said. "And trust me, honey, it won't be a beautiful thing. Let's just say I learned a few new tricks while I was away."

She trusted he'd follow through on that threat. What could

she do? Gage had offered to marry her, but now she knew for certain that wouldn't stop Santo. He'd simply kill her father, kill Gage even, and then take her.

She couldn't appeal to Santo. And she couldn't risk her father's or Gage's life.

A shudder passed through her as her only option became clear.

She wanted to vomit at the very thought.

She didn't have any other choice. She'd finally found a man she could love, he'd even agreed to marry her, and she couldn't have him.

She had to marry Santo.

But she'd make him a deal first. She'd marry him on one condition. His father had to release hers from whatever business arrangement they had. Then she'd destroy the flash drive. It was the only way to ensure her father stayed out of jail. It was the only way to ensure nothing happened to Gage.

If Giovanni agreed to cut all ties with her father, and it appeared as though they'd deleted every piece of evidence that could bring the police to her father's doorstep, then they couldn't hold him. Neither could the police.

She'd have to lie to Gage to defend her father.

She'd have to live her days with a man she despised to save her father.

She'd have to give up the only man she loved to protect her father.

She'd have to give up her choice for love, and her life.

Chapter Twenty-Three

GAGE CROUCHED IN THE ALLEY NEXT TO WADE WHILE they waited for one of their guys on the inside to open the door and let them in. He was pissed. Fuck, he was beyond the simply pissed off point. He was boiling mad.

Lena had promised to call him. After waiting over twenty-four hours, in which she'd managed to avoid him, even arranging for another car service, she'd finally answered her phone.

She'd told him she'd talked to her father, and after tonight's soiree, he would turn himself and the flash drive over to the police. When he'd pressed for details of their conversation, she'd offered nothing. She remained cool and detached. Like she didn't care for him at all.

Her tone and behavior aside, something had felt off. When he'd asked about Santo, she'd brushed his concern off and told him she'd confronted Santo, telling him she had no intention of marrying him. She'd said he wasn't happy, but he finally gave in. Gage no longer needed to marry her to protect her. But she thanked him for offering.

First, Santo Soranno would not say okay and walk away. Not that easy. Therefore, she'd lied. And *thank you for offering*? What the fuck was that about?

Gage had a very bad feeling.

When he'd shown up to take Vincent to the party, Mary had informed him that Vincent and Angelena had already left. She'd thought he'd known. Hell, she'd thought he'd taken them. He'd called Wade and they'd hauled ass downtown. Now they were waiting to be let in.

Finally, the back door creaked open and a blond head stuck out. "Is there a pizza delivery guy out here?"

Wade and Gage stood, brushed dirt off their pants and hurried over to where Pete, one of their best technicians, held the door open.

"Sorry, no pizza tonight," Wade said.

Pete looked disgusted. "It was the least you could do. Fuck, man, I'm starving. Do you know how long I've been hiding in here?"

They brushed past him, slapping him on the shoulder. "I'm sure there will be plenty of stuff to sample at the shindig."

"Yeah, but I'm not dressed to join the party. Nice try imitating Bond by the way." He snorted his laughter. "And Bond wouldn't say shindig."

"Hey," Wade said, "I look pretty awesome in a suit. My mom says so."

Any other time, Gage would have joked along with them, but his inner alarm bells were pinging loudly. "Cut it out, guys. We have work to do."

They followed Pete to the seventh floor, sticking to the shadows, and ducking into empty stairwells or empty rooms if they came across anybody who might question their existence.

"Any problems?" he asked Pete when they were alone.

"Nah. We've watched them sweep the floor twice. We even stashed a few fakes for them to find. Our guess is they're going to meet in Vincent's office. They've been in there multiple times."

"Is there a place to hide?"

"He's got a coat closet and there's an adjoining office. I moved a plant he keeps in front of the door to that room slightly to give us space if you want to hide in the other office. The foliage will give you additional cover when opening that door."

"Perfect. Wade can hide in there and block the outer door from any unwanted visitors. I'll hide in the coat closet."

Pete nodded. "While you guys are scanning the party goers, we'll set up fresh eyes and ears in both places and make sure security doesn't get a chance to get in there and retrieve them before the meeting."

"Where are the others?" There were three more men from his department in the building somewhere.

"Around," was all Pete would say.

They'd reached the floor and Gage peeked into the hall, making sure it was clear. "Ready to join the festivities, Wade?"

"I'm hungry. Let's go get us some escargot."

"Bastards." Pete grumbled and slipped through the door, heading down the hall to Vincent's office.

Gage and Wade knew exactly where it was since they'd been there numerous times under the guise of florists or maintenance men, even security personnel.

For now, he stepped out of the stairwell and turned in the opposite direction. As he walked, he adjusted the lapels on his dinner jacket, heading down the hall to join the party in the main boardroom.

Gage entered the spacious room and his gaze immediately locked on Angelena over in the far the corner with her father. She looked stunning in a long red dress, pearls circling her gorgeous neck. Tonight she'd left her hair down and his fingers itched to feel the silky softness.

221

She watched him. From this distance, he couldn't decipher the look, but she'd noticed him as soon as he'd entered. She'd stiffened, and after a moment, she'd dragged her gaze from his and whispered in her father's ear, distracting him from a conversation he was having with an older couple.

"Over there." Wade nudged him.

Gage pulled his own lustful stare away and looked in the direction his partner indicated on the other side of the room.

There stood both Santo and Giovanni Soranno. Giovanni was engaged in a conversation with a middle-aged well-dressed man with salt and pepper hair. Judging by the way Giovanni leaned in and the tightness of the other man's posture, the conversation wasn't a pleasant one.

It was Santo that actually interested Gage more at the moment. He'd never seen him in person but recognized him from a photo they had. Santo only had eyes for Angelena. And they didn't look friendly at all. The man leered at her.

Gage took a step forward, planning to have a little chat with the wannabe groom.

Wade jerked him back into place. "What the hell do you think you're doing?" he asked between clenched teeth.

Gage swung his head toward his friend, but he didn't pull his attention from Santo for a second. "Looking out for Lena."

"She'll be fine as long as she stays in this room with her father. Now let's split up and try to get closer to Giovanni to see if we can catch anything he says."

Wade gave him a hard look before sauntering away, pausing to snag a drink from a young man holding an almost empty tray of wine glasses. Wade tossed him one more look and then began to make his way toward the Sorannos.

Gage copied his partner, but he headed toward Lena. When

she spotted him, fear blazed across her face and her gaze flew over to Santo. She knew he was watching her. Good. She was on her toes. Gage would simply offer a little more assurance.

Silently, he strolled up to her and her father and waited until the older couple turned away.

Vincent looked shocked to see him. "Gage, what are you doing here?"

"Just wanted to let you know, sir, that whenever you're ready to head home, I won't be far away. I'll be waiting for you in case you need me." Gage hoped he'd conveyed the same message to Lena.

She lowered her eyes and sipped her wine.

"Thank you, Gage. It will be at least a couple of hours. Feel free to enjoy some food though while you wait."

"I will, Mr. Bianco, thank you." She hadn't told her father about him.

Just to ensure she understood, he stepped next to her and while her father spoke with another guest, Gage leaned low and whispered in her ear, "I'm not sure what's going on, Lena, but I need you to know I'm here and I'm not alone. You're safe."

She peered up at him, her tone pleading. "Please leave me alone, Gage. I don't want to give him the wrong impression."

"Santo? Did you not tell him you weren't marrying him?"

Her eyes shifted away. "I've convinced my father to go to the police," she whispered. "I'll find you tomorrow morning and we can go then."

"I thought we were getting married tomorrow morning?" It had all been part of the plan to keep her out of Santo's clutches. They'd discussed going to courthouse. He'd found himself looking forward to it.

"I already told you, that won't be necessary now, Gage. You don't have to worry. I've got everything taken care of." She gasped.

He jerked his head up, connecting with Santo's glare. Santo's eyes gleamed with hate. A vicious snarl curled his lip.

"Please, Gage. Let me handle this."

Not likely. He wasn't letting her or her father out of his sight.

Santo stepped forward.

Gage reluctantly moved away. Wade had been right. As long as Lena and her father stayed in this room, they'd be fine.

* * *

Lena sighed in relief when Gage wandered away, dressed to kill and looking like he belonged in this crowd.

As soon he and his friend had entered the conference room, it was like a beacon had gone off over the door and a big flashing neon arrow directly over Gage's head.

If only it were that simple.

She'd also known exactly where Santo was. Every inch that man moved, she zeroed in on his position. She hadn't looked at him directly once, but she'd been more than aware of him. Thankfully, his father's presence appeared to be keeping him in line, because neither of them had spoken to her or her father yet. In fact, it was almost as if they were avoiding one another.

Which suited her just fine. She didn't want to be near them. It was bad enough she had to be here at all, but her father had refused to cancel. There was no way she'd leave him on his own, risking that he might say or do something that would alert Giovanni too soon.

Her father didn't know about the flash drive, or the fact that she planned to negotiate with Santo and his father. She was still trying to come to terms with the fact that she intended to go through with the wedding, but only if Santo promised not to hurt her father.

"Hey, baby."

How did Santo cross the room without her noticing? Panic raced through her. The hair on the back of her neck stood at attention. She'd taken her eyes off him for one moment. She immediately searched for Gage. He was on the far side of the room talking to Wade. They both watched Giovanni like a hawk. Even from where she stood, she noticed the tension in their bodies. Both men had strangle holds on the drinks they held, but neither sipped a drop. She turned her head slightly only to find her father had stepped away and was looking at something one of his associates held.

"Come with me." Santo whispered the command in her ear.

"No."

"Yes." He gripped her elbow, his fingers digging into her flesh.

Wincing, she tried to make it appear as though she were leaving of her own accord, when in reality he dragged her.

The hallway held few people so he easily ushered her down the hall. She knew the only office open on this floor would be her father's as she'd been in there earlier, so it was no surprise when he pushed her though the door and slammed it closed behind him. She prayed somebody heard the noise.

He let her loose and she backed up until she hit her father's desk.

"I'm pretty sure I told you no talking to other men." Santo stalked her.

She refused to cower or show him fear. "That was my father's driver. He was just letting us know where he'd be parked when it was time to leave."

He ran a hand down her cheek, and then around to the back of her neck. "I don't care who he is. Nobody talks to my wife without my permission." He gripped her neck in a tight squeeze.

She couldn't keep the whimper from tumbling past her lips. "You're hurting me."

"You're mine to hurt."

"I'm not yours yet," she clarified.

"A few days won't make a difference."

"I want to make a deal with you, Santo."

Surprise lit up his dark eyes. Then he laughed. "You want to make a deal with me? Okay, babe. What are you offering?" He loosened his hold slightly.

"I will marry you if you promise to get your father to fire mine and leave him be. I don't want my father working for yours anymore."

Santo squinted. "My old man's not going to let his accountant go just like that. Sorry. No deal."

She felt tears well, but she pushed them back. She had to get him to agree. "If he doesn't I'll go to the police."

He barked out a harsh laugh. "With what? What could you possibly have that would force my father to do anything you want, besides kill you and your old man."

"Information. I have my father's files. All of them. I'll hand all of it over to the police. I swear."

He let her go, retreated a few steps, and placed his hands

on his hips as he assessed her up and down. "I don't believe you."

She swallowed. "I have it all on a thumb drive. Every offshore account, every fake business, every transaction over the last twenty-five years."

He narrowed his eyes. "Prove it."

The door opened and her father poked his head around the corner. "Angelena, what are you doing in here?" Her father stepped into his office, caught sight of Santo and stopped in his tracks. "Is everything okay?" He looked back and forth between them.

"I'm fine, Papa."

"Get your ass in here, *Papa*. We need to have a little chat."

Her father slowly moved further into the room and closed the door. He edged around the space until he stood next to her. "What do you want?"

"Your daughter here tells me she has all your files and she plans to hand them over to the police unless I get my father to release you from his employ."

Her father's head whipped around as he stared at her in shock.

"I told Santo I'd marry him if he'd get his father to let you go. If they won't, I'll turn everything over to the police myself."

Every single year of his life appeared on his face, as well as a flurry of emotion. Surprise. Sadness. Regret. Fear. Resignation. Then he bent forward. He pressed his lips to her forehead. "I love you, Angelena," he whispered for her ears only.

Tears gathered. Why would he say that now? Her heart pounded.

Her father stepped in front of her. "Santo. My daughter will not be marrying you. I want her to marry a man she loves and one who loves her."

Santo seemed to grow larger.

He stepped closer and his hand came out from behind his back. He held a gun. Pointed right at her father.

"No!" She tried to shove her father aside and place herself in front of him, but he held her arm tight, his strength surprising her. She struggled, but he refused to release her. She laid her head against his shoulder for a second and then clung to his arm as they both faced the man who would kill them.

"I plan to have your daughter, old man. I don't care if I have to shoot you to make it happen. My father can always find another accountant." He raised the gun.

"Drop it, Santo."

All of them swung their heads around. Gage stood in the adjoining doorway, a gun trained on Santo. The main door opened and Wade slipped in. He also held a gun.

"Gage. How did you—"

"When I realized you and Santo were missing, I took a chance I'd find you here. I've been listening from the other room." He darted a quick glance toward her father. "I'm happy to hear you're reneging on the marriage thing, Mr. Bianco. I don't think Santo is the right man for your daughter."

Her poor father looked so confused. "You don't?"

"Nope. But I am."

She whirled around. What did that mean? Did he care for her? Did he love her? Did he really want to marry her? What the hell was going on?

"I can see the questions in your eyes, honey. I promise we'll work them all out later." Gage turned back to Santo, who had stepped closer to her and her father.

"I wouldn't do that, Soranno."

"You're not going to kill me." He sneered. "There's a room full of people just down the hall."

"Try me. I'm not worried about the attention. In fact, I hope it brings your father running. We could have a little party down here before I haul you both off to jail."

Santo grunted. He flashed a look in her direction. His features were calm. Too calm. She saw it in his eyes a second before he raised his arm, the gun pointing straight at her father's head.

He grinned, the look pure evil.

There was a loud bang, an odd smell, and when she looked down, Santo lay on the floor, blood pooling from beneath the side of his head, his dead eyes staring straight ahead.

Her ears were ringing.

She looked up at Gage.

He released his grip on his gun and dropped his arm down to his side.

The reality of the situation settled in. It was as though the entire room erupted in one collective gasp. Or was that just her?

Her legs collapsed, but her father caught her before she hit the floor and then she found herself in Gage's arms.

He squeezed her tight and then reared back. He cupped her face, and stared intently into her eyes. His were wide with alarm. "Are you okay? Did he touch you? Did he hurt you?"

She tried to look at the floor, but Gage blocked her view. "You shot him," she said.

"Yes, Angelena. I did. He'd dead. Are you okay?" he asked again.

"I'm fine. Papa?" She jerked out of Gage's hold and spun around to find her father looking stunned as he first looked at her then down at Santo then back at her. She threw her arms around his neck. "Papa." Oh dear God. Santo had come so close to killing her father.

"It's over, Angelena. Everyone's fine." Her father patted her hair gently.

Lena could not miss the tremble in his hand, in his entire body. Or the fact that it wasn't over yet and not everybody would be fine.

Chapter Twenty-Four

"**M**R. BIANCO." GAGE STEPPED FORWARD. "I'M ACTUally..."

The sound of running feet grew close. Of course, the sound of gunfire had brought security and who knew who else. All he needed was one of the firm's guests tripping over a dead body. He was in the process of pulling his badge from his pocket when Giovanni Soranno made his big entrance.

The door flew open and crashed against the wall. Giovanni stood in the doorway, a couple of large and imposing men behind him, not part of the building's security team.

Giovanni's gaze jumped around the room, took in the situation, and then landed on his son lying on the floor. His chest heaved. His jaw hardened. Soranno raised his head, his eyes narrowing on him and then Vincent, before jumping back to him again.

Rage flared in Giovanni's face, his skin mottled in red. When his eyes darted back to Gage's hand, he looked ready to explode. He pinned a deadly stare on Vincent. His hands were fisted at his sides and he looked like a snorting bull pawing the ground, ready to charge.

"You brought the police into this, Vincent?" Giovanni shook his head, slowly. "Not a wise move my friend." He slipped one hand behind his back.

Gage stepped between Soranno and Lena's father. From the corner of his eye, he saw Wade creeping closer.

Voices in the hall headed in their direction and a woman yelled that the police and an ambulance had arrived.

Gage saw Giovanni glance to the floor. A flash of sadness, or maybe regret, crossed his face, and then he spun and ran out the door.

"I've got him." Wade tried to follow but the two big men in the doorway stopped him. "This is a police matter. Get out of his way," Wade yelled.

By the time his partner managed to shove his way past security, the police had arrived, and a crowd had gathered in the hallway.

Giovanni was gone.

"Grab the others and search the building," Gage told his frustrated partner. He understood the feeling. After all this time and they'd had him, only to let him get away.

Wade left to deal with business. Lena and her father stood huddled on the other side of his desk as far from Santo's body as they could be without actually leaving the room. The emergency response team confirmed no vitals and prepared to bag the body. The police had started questioning people.

When he'd realized she'd left the boardroom, his heart had lodged in his throat. Panic had set in. He'd given no thought whatsoever to Giovanni, who had still been in the board-room, chatting up a couple of professionals, trying to act as if he belonged among decent law-abiding people.

Giovanni's degenerate son had been missing, and so had Lena. Gage had hurried out of the room. Pure instinct had urged him down the hall toward Vincent's office. Hearing voices inside, he'd snuck into the adjoining office where he'd overheard their conversation and then Vincent joining them.

He knew Santo had hurt her. He'd heard her whimper and

had to hold himself back from barging through the door, his gun blazing. The only time he'd been as scared as he was tonight was the night his brother died and he'd left his family home.

It was time to come clean with Lena about who he was. It was time to tell her he loved her.

Gage finished giving his statement to the men in charge and waited until both Lena and her father had given theirs.

Wade returned and waved him over. "He got away."

"You checked everywhere? He's not hiding in the building somewhere?"

Wade shook his head. "I have the guys looking again, but we turned up nothing on the first round."

Damn. Honestly, he wasn't surprised. "We'll get him." Gage felt confident about that. It would just take a little more time. "Hang around, will you?"

Wade glanced at Lena and her father. "Sure. Let me know when you're ready."

Now came the other hard part of the evening. He didn't, for one minute, regret killing Santo. Shockingly, he didn't even regret not catching Giovanni. But this, he did regret. He didn't want to see Lena hurt. He knew what he had to do now would definitely cause her great pain. A pain no doctor could fix.

Gage walked over to where she stood with Vincent, their hands clasped together, hanging on to each other as though they were about to be ripped apart.

As he approached, they booth looked up from where they'd had their heads bent, their discussion just between the two of them.

"Gage. Or is it Officer Barrett?" Vincent asked.

"Gage is fine."

"Did you get Giovanni?" Lena asked.

"No."

Fear sparked in her brown eyes. Fear Gage wanted to see gone, and he planned to do everything in his power to ensure it went away and stayed away. "Don't worry. We'll get him."

"So you've been undercover this entire time?" Vincent asked.

"Yes, sir."

"And it's during this time you fell in love with my daughter?"

Lena spun to stare wide-eyed at her father. "Papa!"

Gage chuckled. "Yes, sir."

She swiveled back and stared at him. "Gage?"

"Do you promise to look after her while I'm away?"

"Oh, Papa." Tears choked her up.

Gage wanted nothing more than to take her in his arms and comfort her, knowing that the next number of days would be some of the longest and hardest of her life. "I promise, sir. I won't let anything happened to her."

Vincent turned and faced his daughter. He took both her hands in his and looked deep into her eyes as though memorizing her.

He should let them have this moment, but he couldn't bring himself to let her out of his sight again.

"Angelena, you are strong. I wish your mother could have known you. I am so proud of you."

"Papa, please."

"Hush. Gage is a good man. I trust him. He'll take care of you. He'll love you."

"But Papa…"

"Do you love him, Angelena?"

Gage held his breath, not entirely sure how he'd react if she didn't say yes.

"I do, Papa. I love Gage."

"Do you want to be with him? Is this the man you'd chose to be your husband?"

Lena swept her pretty eyes up and looked straight into his. Hers glistened with tears. But they overflowed with love. Love for him.

"Yes. He's most definitely my first choice."

Vincent wiped away the tears racing down her cheeks. A few had begun to fall from his as well. He kissed his daughter. Then he released her right hand and dug into his pocket. He held a black flash drive out to Gage, never taking his eyes from his daughter.

"Everything you need is on here. My daughter had only copied from my home computer, but I've given you what I have here as well. You'll find all the accounts, the businesses, and the transfers are well documented. I've made notes as well. I've named names where I could." He paused and glanced at Gage before returning to Lena. "I needed insurance, just in case anything happened to me."

Lena sobbed and fell into her father's arms.

Vincent peered at Gage over his shoulder, tears dripping down his aged cheeks. "Please don't let anything happened to her, Gage. She's all I have."

"I won't, Mr. Bianco. I love her with all my heart. I'll protect her with my life."

"That's all I can ask."

Epilogue

THIS DAY WAS NOT TURNING OUT AT ALL AS SHE'D IMAG-
ined.

Angelena stood at the back of the small chapel, in the front
foyer waiting for her cue to enter. Outside, darkness crept
in and an early snowfall blanketed the ground, slickened the
streets, and left the air crisp enough that each exhale frosted
the air. To her left, a six-foot Christmas tree adorned with
hand-crafted ornaments blinked its rainbow of colors.

Her dress, a simple but elegant long sheath-wedding gown
in white chiffon with a sheer lace back, molded her body to
perfection, the bottom puddling in a small circle around her
feet. She clutched a small bouquet of white roses and baby's
breath. Her hands trembled.

She wished with her whole heart that her father were at
her side. After all they'd been through, he was the only family
she had, the only one to witness the biggest day of her life.
He should be standing beside her as she prepared to take this
next step in her life. A step she never thought she'd take. Not
for real anyway.

She'd spoken with him this morning, needing to get the
tears out of the way before she committed herself forever
to one man. The sorrow and regret in his voice had ripped
through her, shattering her calm, stealing some of the happi-
ness she'd been harboring for the last few days. He knew
Gage loved her. He trusted the man she loved. And he agreed
with her choice of husband.

Inside the chapel, behind the doors currently closed in front of her, the organ began to play, benches creaked, clothing rustled and feet shuffled as those in attendance stood, waiting for the bride's big entrance.

Months ago when she'd sat in her father's home office, stunned to discover she was to be married, she'd thrown a tantrum no different than that of a young child. She'd been adamant that she would not abide by her father's wishes. There was no way in hell she would marry a man not of her choosing.

So much had changed since then.

Her father was in protective custody, heading into witness protection. Other than one far too short telephone call today, all other communications had been through the authorities. She'd been assured he was being cared for and in no immediate danger. But she wouldn't be able to see or speak to him for a very long time.

Her would-be husband was thankfully dead. Her would-be father-in-law, unfortunately, was nowhere to be found. Giovanni had skipped town. He'd left his son lying in a pool of blood and her father hanging as the scapegoat for his crimes.

Rosa had disappeared too, but Lena knew it was on her own accord and that she was safe. Lena had called home that night to tell her what had happened, that her brother was dead and her father gone. By the time she'd arrived home, Rosa was gone. She checked in every few weeks, but wouldn't tell Lena where she was. It was probably for the best.

The organ music hit a crescendo. The solid oak double doors with the intricate scrollwork inlay would be opening any second now.

Her mind drifted to her mother, a woman she barely remembered. Angelena had to believe her mother would be proud of her today. Even though things didn't work out as her father had planned, Angelena had remained firm in her resolve. Along the way, she'd uncovered some truths about him and his business dealings that had her mother been alive, never would have happened. Their lives would have been so different.

She wouldn't be here today, about to marry the man of her heart.

She also believed her mother would forgive her father for his error in judgment and the mistakes he'd made. Considering the circumstances, Angelena was on her way to forgiving him, but she wasn't quite there yet. He'd put himself, and her, at risk.

And if he hadn't had a strike of good conscience at the last minute, with lots of urging from her, one or both of them could very well be dead right now.

The doors opened, the squeak of the hinges barely registering as she raised her head and looked down the aisle.

There he was.

He looked handsome in a uniform.

He looked delicious out of one.

But he totally rocked a tuxedo.

His family turned and watched her glide down the aisle, moving ever closer to Gage. That was the one good thing to come out of this whole mess. Gage had begun to make peace with his family. She still didn't understand the whole story. Only that after Giovanni killed Gage's brother, he had distanced himself, laying the blame at his own feet for the murder and doing everything he could to bring down men like the one who'd gunned down an innocent teenage boy.

His father and sister beamed. His mother wiped tears from her eyes as she swept her gaze back and forth between her son and his wife to be. Angelena looked forward to getting to know them. With her own father in hiding somewhere, she welcomed the family she'd inherited.

She settled her gaze on her soon-to-be-husband.

Gage. He only had eyes for her. His gaze had found and locked onto hers the moment she'd cleared the entryway. The light, the passion, and the love shining there, all for her, only for her, made her feel light as air. She floated down the aisle toward him.

His family sat on one side, his friends on the other, balancing out the room. She was speechless at their thoughtfulness. Mary smiled with the pride of a parent, bringing tears to Lena's eyes.

The sound of the organ quieted the whispers of their handful of guests. She heard her heart beating. Beating for the man she loved.

Finally, she came to rest beside him.

"You look stunning, Angelena." His soft words thrilled her. She smile warmed her.

"So do you." She wanted to reach out and run her hands all over him. She wanted to look at every angle of the custom-tailored suit and then she wanted to rip it off him and look at every angle of her husband in the flesh. Her mouth watered and she moaned.

Gage groaned low enough only she could hear, loud enough the rumble sent a fiery charge through her bloodstream.

Twenty minutes. Twenty minutes and they'd be husband

and wife. Twenty minutes and she could do whatever she wanted to this sexy man.

To the one she'd risked her life to be with. The one she'd chosen to be her temporary stand-in husband so she wouldn't have to say I do to a criminal intent on destroying her, if he didn't actually kill her first.

To the man who'd quickly become so much more than a stand-in. He'd become the one she willingly wanted to spend the rest of her life with, no matter how long that life happened to be.

To the man who, when given a choice, chose her.

And she, most definitely, chose him.

~ * ~ * ~

Family Ties, Book 2

She didn't fit the family mold. But she fit him perfectly.

Wade and Rosa's Story
Coming in 2017

About the Author

Shoes are her addiction, but books are her passion. Anne reads many genres of romance, but prefers to write sexy stories about characters you can relate to, and always with a side of those sinful pleasures your mom never told you about.

While embarking on this wild journey of being a romance author, Anne juggles a full time job and a family. She grew up in Southern Ontario, Canada, but now makes her home in Eastern Ontario where she lives with her wonderfully supportive husband, three awesome kids, Rocky the bearded dragon, and Lily the chocolate lab.

Discover more about Anne Lange here:

Web Site
http://authorannelange.com/

Facebook
https://www.facebook.com/AuthorAnneLange

Twitter (@Anne_Lange)
https://twitter.com/Anne_Lange

Goodreads
http://www.goodreads.com/author/show/6896566.Anne_Lange

Newsletter:
https://app.mailerlite.com/webforms/landing/e1o4u7

Check out the first books in Anne's other series

FRIENDS WITH BENEFITS
THE VAULT SERIES

Can sexual exploration lead to three times the bliss?

Tyler had no idea his wife Angela's desires so closely matched his own. But when some unguarded pillow talk reveals her fantasy of two men at once, Tyler jumps at the chance to make her happy.

Enlisting the help of his best friend Connor, who'd shared some threesome adventures with him in the past, Tyler secretly hopes exploring Angela's fantasies will lead to his own personal desire—a permanent threesome with the two people he loves most in the world.

Connor can't believe it when his best friend asks him to seduce his wife. Then he meets Angela, and all the women in his past fade away. With Tyler's blessing, Connor sets out to melt Angela's reserve, and when Tyler joins the party, the three of them set the sheets on fire.

Angela is floored when her husband suggests they explore some of her fantasies—things she'd only read about but never in a million years thought she'd actually do. Sandwiched between Tyler and Connor, she's never felt so treasured, so protected, so loved.

But the reality proves much more complicated than the fantasy. She loves her husband, but she finds herself falling for his best friend too. That's not normal, is it? What will people think?

SLIDING INTO HOME
A NEW LEAGUE SERIES

Can an injured ex ball player convince the woman he wakes up married to in Las Vegas to take a second chance on him?

After spending the last four months drowning his sorrows over the end of his baseball career, Jack Bishop finds himself winging through the blue skies to Las Vegas, not so ready to spend the weekend with some woman his best friend set him up with. He expects a paid escort. What he gets is the woman he walked away from ten years ago to pursue his passion, and she's not very happy to see him.

Devyn Tate believes she's quite capable of finding somebody to take her out to dinner. She's no longer looking for a lifelong promise. She has a commitment only to her battery-operated toy to fulfill that particular need. Yet her friends have managed to talk her into spending the weekend in Las Vegas, on a blind date of all things. They promise the guy is trustworthy. They insist that she should have fun. Unfortunately, fun is not what she envisions when she discovers Jack Bishop lying on the floor of her suite in nothing but his underwear that's on backward, and she has a wedding ring on her finger.

CHECK YOUR INHIBITIONS
AT THE DOOR. . .

Anne
LANGE

WWW.AUTHORANNELANGE.COM

hotRom publishing

www.ingramcontent.com/pod-product-compliance
Lightning Source LLC
Chambersburg PA
CBHW021234250626
47155CB00008B/3004